D1563339

AFRICAN WRITERS SERIES

Editorial Adviser · Chinua Achebe

70

Chief the Honourable Minister

AFRICAN WRITERS SERIES

Chief the Honourable Minister

◇

T. M. Aluko

Ofolorunso

HEINEMANN

LONDON IBADAN NAIROBI

Heinemann Educational Books Ltd
48 Charles Street, London W1 X8AH
PMB 5205 IBADAN · POB 25080 NAIROBI
EDINBURGH MELBOURNE TORONTO AUCKLAND
HONG KONG SINGAPORE NEW DELHI

ISBN 0 435 90070 6

Printed in Great Britain by
Cox & Wyman Ltd, London, Fakenham and Reading

One

---◇---

THE Prime Minister of the newly independent state of Afromacoland beamed a long-distance smile at his visitor. 'Ah, Moses' he said in a sing-song voice, as he rose from the big executive chair behind the massive mahogany desk at the other end of the room. 'Welcome back from your tour.'

'Thank you, sir,' Alade Moses muttered, shaking the hand the Prime Minister offered him.

'I am glad I'm now able to offer to you in person my congratulations on your victory in the Newtown North Constituency,' the Prime Minister continued still holding Moses' hand. 'And on your appointment as a Minister of State.'

'Thank you, sir.'

'This way, Minister, this way,' the Prime Minister said as he piloted his visitor in an urbane manner to an oval-shaped side table round which were ranged six easy chairs. Into one of these he waved Moses after he had himself sat down in another. 'Your victory is the more gratifying judging by the activities of Dauda and his gang. I understand that they were absolutely sure they would win the seat. Indeed, I understand that Dauda took a £500 bet on the issue.'

'So I hear, sir. And that Geo Abyssinia is already after him for the £500.'

'A measure of the trust your people have in your Improvement Union. I understand that they have a tremendous influence on the chiefs and people of Newtown. Amazing how much influence for good these tribal unions can be if their activities are canalized into profitable channels. Your people in Newtown have set the rest of us in the country an example to follow, Moses. I hope we shall follow it,' he declared, looking straight into the eyes of his visitor.

'But, sir —' Moses started, and then stopped.

'Yes?'

'I really don't know how to put it, sir. I just can't think. I'm – I'm – I'm just confused by the whole thing.'

'Confused, really? I'm sure you are no more than awed by the burden of State which you have now been called upon to bear.'

'Yes, sir. You see —'

'Your reaction, Moses' – the Prime Minister cut him short – 'is quite understandable, the approach of the man of intellect and ability to responsibility. But you must be up and doing at once. There's so much work to be done. There are so few of us to do it.'

Moses thought that the Prime Minister paused for him to say something at this point. 'Thirty-six hours ago, I was in London. The day before that I was in Bristol, on the delegation visiting schools. Now today I'm here, sir. I'm to abandon the Grammar School, sir. And —'

'My dear Moses, the more you express these views the more I admire you. I admire your devotion to the school for which you have done so much in so short a time.' Here the Prime Minister pointed Moses to a packet of cigarettes on the table. 'It is precisely your success in the management of this comparatively local institution that has pointed to the need to use your great talent and energy for service at the national level.'

One of the four telephones on the big desk rang. The Prime Minister contemplated it for some time, apparently debating in his mind whether or not he should attend to it. Then he got up and strode back to his desk, picking up the telephone.

Meanwhile, Moses made a furtive survey of the room. He was impressed by its sheer size – it was as big as the assembly hall of his Grammar School. The furniture was of a quality which he had never seen before. The flat tops of the conference table at which he sat, of the desk at which the Prime Minister was now phoning, and of the occasional table at the other corner were all finished in some material which made them shine like glass. It was obvious to him that this was more than the effect of polish on mahogany, which showed well on the arms and legs of the chairs and tables. The seats of the chairs looked like expensive woollen material but had the feel of rubber. The entire floor was covered with a red carpet. Two air-conditioners droned rather noisily in the external wall. The whole place was cool, nearly cold, and rather solemn. This could have been a room in Buckingham Palace in London or in the White House in Washington, he thought. This was where the British Governor had thrown his last spanners into the momentum-gathering movement for self-government – and lost. The post had now been abolished, the last incumbent transferred (on promotion) to East Africa, and his office now occupied by the first African Prime Minister.

From the splendour of the room his mind went to its owner still speaking on the telephone. He noticed that his big robe and trousers of cream gaberdine were newly laundered and that the sleeves of the jumper were fastened with gold links as in a dress shirt. He wore a long gold chain round his neck and the black and red badge of the

3

Freedom For All Party outside the breast pocket of his robe. His hair was black, and plentiful. Moses thought that he no doubt applied some dye to keep it black. In his brown, heeled shoes, he stood six feet plus.

Then the real person before him dissolved in Moses' mind. In his stead, Moses saw Christopher Bandele Ogun the surgeon, in a white overall, sweating over the unconscious form of his patient on the theatre table. He remembered how this famous politician and medical practitioner had divided the whole of his adulthood between acquiring medical qualifications and fighting British imperialism. He recalled the typical student article he, Moses, had written in the *West African Review* three years before in which he had attacked a speech Dr Band-Ogun was reported to have made at a Rotary Club luncheon during a short lecture tour of Britain. Several African students in Britain had considered the speech an outrage, a sell-out of the African cause. Moses himself had not joined in the student demonstration at Hyde Park but he had written to attack 'the so-called nationalists who find difficulty in controlling their tongues after dining and wining with the agents of imperialism'. He had urged the erring nationalist to hurry from London to Liverpool and take the first available boat back home to Victoria. 'And on landing in Victoria let him hurry to the African Church Cathedral on the Marina at which we know he is a devout worshipper. There let him confess his manifold sins and wickedness. There let him ask for God's forgiveness for this abominable crime against his own kind. Finally, let him retire to his surgery and devote the rest of his useful life to the curing of the sick. May he be a greater success at this than he has been in the field of politics.' He was wondering if the Chief remembered this article and if he connected him with it.

He was still lost in contemplation of this embarrassing and sole link between him and the Prime Minister when he

4

noticed that the latter had finished on the telephone and was already addressing him from his desk. 'For this reason at least, we are under obligation to select a Minister from your Constituency,' the Prime Minister was now saying. 'I am happy to say, however, that your choice only happens to coincide with our political desire to have a Newtown man in the Cabinet. I would make you a Minister of State any day irrespective of what constituency you came from, Moses. Men of high intellectual attainment and integrity are rare in our society. Such of them as we can find must not be allowed to run to waste. We must utilize them to the utmost.'

Again the telephone rang. But this time, the Prime Minister ignored it. He went on contemplating his visitor critically: 'In this first truly all-African Cabinet I want only men of ability and character. This was why I told the Party boys to shut their traps when someone quoted Article 3a of the Party's Charter in respect of ministerial appointments. In normal circumstances, you could not be appointed a Minister of State without your loyalty to the Party having been tested over a minimum period of three years.'

The Prime Minister paused. He rose and took a few long strides to the window. Moses was fascinated at the way the heavy curtains parted in the middle when the Chief pulled the brass ball dangling on the end of a cord.

'Looks like another storm, eh?' The Prime Minister observed, looking through the window.

'Just so, sir,' Moses confirmed as he too studied the disposition of the clouds from where he sat.

'Isn't it strange, in a pleasant sort of way, that the moment you and I see this particular arrangement of clouds in the sky, and the direction in which this particular one is drifting we know there's going to be a storm?'

'Yes, sir.'

'Our fathers for many generations back knew these things. They knew which formation of clouds would produce a thunderstorm. They could order from the clouds electricity to be delivered by the god Shango to the house of their enemy. Yet the imperialists say we have no civilization in Africa . . . You wait, Moses. When the new University of Afromacoland is established, it will be heavily endowed for research in African super-science, derogatorily called juju by those who do not like us —'

He was interrupted by the buzzing of the intercom.

'Yes, who? I am meeting H.E. at 11.30. That's another forty-five minutes – no, fifty-five,' he said slowly scanning the gold watch on his left wrist. 'I've already seen the Minister of Agriculture and the Minister of Education. The Minister of Works is with me now. That makes three. I think I can see another three before the appointment with H.E. That means Economic Development, Trade and Industry, and Information. Who? Minister of Chieftaincy Affairs? No, not till tomorrow. So put him and the other – er – three Ministers for tomorrow morning, starting at 10 a.m. Fifteen minutes to each Minister. . . . Now you should tell His Highness that I'll see him – let's see now – at 1 p.m. No, no. I don't want to see him till I've seen the Minister of Chieftaincy Affairs. Look, tell His Highness that the Minister of Chieftaincy Affairs will see him now and that I will see both of them tomorrow. Good.'

As he went to switch off one of the two air conditioners he said: 'I think I was saying how happy I am to be able to meet the wishes of your people in Newtown and at the same time to have as colleague a man of your ability and character.'

'You flatter me, sir.'

'I do not flatter people, Minister. I say to their face what I'd say behind their back. That was why I got your case through the Party Caucus easily.'

'Thank you, sir.'

'Incidentally, I understand that the vicar of your church

6

preached a powerful sermon at the Thanksgiving Service yesterday. I'm sorry I wasn't there, but I hear many people were nearly moved to tears when he was recounting your achievements. I'm glad that your people have learnt to put first things first by thanking God for our victory at the polls.'

'Yes, sir,' Moses muttered.

'Just one more thing. Moses, I decided to make you Minister of Works against advice and criticism.'

'Yes, sir?'

'I want a strong man in that Ministry. We must prosecute a heavy programme of development in our first five-year term of office. We must in those five years do more than the British did in fifty years of colonial rule. And this is not just an empty boast. I mean it. I must have someone with drive and imagination in that Ministry. That's why I selected you for this assignment.'

'Thank you, sir. But I thought I would go to Education,' Moses said hardly concealing his perplexity. 'I know nothing about engineering.'

'That's just the point, Minister. You don't have to know anything about engineering. You see, you don't have to be an authority on education to be Minister of Education or a physician or surgeon to be Minister of Health. The experts are all there to help you. Your Permanent Secretary is there to advise you. And, by the way, you are to read all the literature you can lay your hand on on parliamentary institutions and procedure, and on the organization of the Civil Service. In particular, read the White Paper on "Integration into Ministries". The responsibilies and relationships of the Minister, the Permanent Secretary, and Professional Officers are all clearly defined there. I have directed that every Minister should be given a copy of it.'

'Yes, sir.'

'Just one thing more, Minister. While you are substantively Minister of Works, you will in fact be our unofficial spokesman on education. An adviser to and cross-check on the Minister of Education. You see what I mean?' He smiled Moses out of the room.

From the 'owner's corner' in the black official station wagon that brought him from the office of the Prime Minister he waved to groups of party supporters who cheered him. He acknowledged the greetings of more supporters and constituency members who crowded both the balcony and the waiting room in his first-floor office in the Ministry of Works.

As he took his seat he noticed that the furniture in his room though of a different design from that in the office of the Prime Minister, was of good quality too. He swivelled round in the big chair behind the massive desk and nodded with satisfaction at the splendour of the whole thing: the artificially produced micro-climate in the room, the up-holstery of the easy chairs, the glossy finish of the top of the side table, and the red carpet that covered the entire floor.

Here he was, Alade Moses, till three days before the Principal of Newtown Grammar School. Today he was a Minister of State. As he had told the Prime Minister, he just was confused by the sudden transformation. He recollected the scene at the Oliver Cromwell Grammar School masters' room exactly three days to the hour when the cable was handed over to him. 'Congratulations stop you are ap-pointed Minister in new government stop Fly home immediately stop Gorgeous Gregory Secretary General Newtown Improvement Union stop.' He recollected how he had had to read the cable again and again before he got its meaning. It had meant his having to tear himself from the party of nine headmasters from Commonwealth countries on five weeks' tour of secondary grammar schools in Britain organized by the British Council. He sighed in genuine embarrassment at the situation he found himself in. Not only had the British Council wasted its

8

money and effort in taking him to Britain to see grammar schools at work in that country with a view to his learning a thing or two that would help him in running his own school back home in Afromacoland, but he must now abandon all his plans for Newtown Grammar School and start on an entirely new career – the career of a politician.

His private secretary came in and told him that a number of people were in the waiting-room to see him. He, however, thought the Minister might like to see the papers first before seeing the callers. He sorted out the papers and placed them in the in-tray, and tiptoed out of the room.

A blue asterisk caught his attention on a front-page leader in the Opposition paper. A frown creased his face as he read it eagerly. He was sure the Prime Minister had not seen that paper before he interviewed him barely twenty minutes before. He read it a second time:

'It was bad enough for these men without conscience to associate the name of the God of Truth with the great fraud that they have committed in their mad ambition to rule this nation at all cost. It was bad enough for them to say that it was God that gave them victory when in fact they know what we know and what the omniscient God knows that they had raped the electoral regulations and bullied corrupt and weak-minded electoral authorities into declaring their candidate returned unopposed. But it is worse for the gates of the house of God – the God of truth – to be thrown open to the perpetrators of this fraud for a so-called thanksgiving service for winning an election which they had rigged. But above all it is a sin against the eternal Creator that an ordained priest of the God of truth could bring himself so low as to preside over such a service of deceit and to say such nice things about a young man who at the last election was persuaded to take the wrong turning, to the road that leads to degradation, depravity, and ruin.'

'Let the vicar of the First Methodist Church, Newtown, return immediately to Alade Moses the contaminating conscience money with which he has attempted to bribe the church at the altar of the First Methodist Church. Thereafter let the vicar arrange for Moses and his gang the Service of Commination which is a pronouncement of God's anger and judgement against sinners who are not yet too far gone in their sin, that they may be punished in this world that their souls may be saved in the world to come. Alade Moses is not yet too far gone in his sin. May God grant him grace to retrace his steps back to the path of righteousness and diligent service to the nation in the field in which he is competent – before it is too late.'

Two

$\diamond$

ALADE MOSES surprised himself at the speed with which he reconciled himself to his new circumstances and got over the upset that Abdul Dauda's attack on him in the Opposition paper had caused him. He took comfort in the knowledge that he had not sought nomination for the election. He was away from the country when the whole thing took place. It was obvious that he could not have been privy to the alleged irregularity in the method of his election to Parliament.

Thirteen days after his arrival from Britain, the Newtown Improvement Union gave him a loud reception. Gorgeous Gregory, Secretary General of the Union, was the Master of Ceremonies and the brain behind it.

'Welcome, Our New Minister', proclaimed banners in red and black at the two gates where the Trunk A road entered and left the town. 'Welcome, Minister Alade Moses of Newtown', 'Newtown is proud of its first Minister son'. These and a number of others were chalked at several points on the tarred surface of the road.

All Newtown had turned up at the lorry park for the occasion. The day had been declared a public holiday for the employees of the Local Authority and the schools in the town and district. It had already caused a row between

Gorgeous Gregory and the District Engineer of the local branch of the Public Works who had refused to declare a holiday for his own staff because he had received no instructions from headquarters that he should do so. All the school children had been marched to the lorry park a couple of hours before the ceremony was due to start, the boys in their smart khaki shirts and shorts and the girls in their blue frocks. The townsfolk were all gaily dressed, the men in their Sunday best of Sanyan suits and carrying their umbrellas, the women in colourful blouses and wrappers and headties, with plenty of trinkets to match. While the school children sang well-known marches the women danced to a combined orchestra of gangan, shekere, and trumpets from the band of the Local Government Police Force.

The clouds gathered threateningly. But Gorgeous Gregory had bade his people to set their hearts at rest. He had paid a large sum of money to the head of the rain-makers cult to see that rain did not come to mar the great occasion.

After several attempts rendered abortive by the great noise of the crowd Gorgeous Gregory eventually succeeded in making a start.

'This is indeed a red letter day in the annals of this great city,' his voice boomed over the loudspeaker.

Moses recalled from where he sat on the platform under a canopy of green canvas, flanked on one side by an empty chair reserved for the Chairman and on the other by one of his ministerial colleagues, that exactly nineteen months before Gorgeous Gregory had declared another day a red letter day in the annals of Newtown. That was the day the Union were holding another reception for him for his safe return from his studies in Britain and for his appointment as Principal of the local Grammar School.

Again, there was a temporary setback in the proceedings

as some commotion in the crowd appeared to be spreading rapidly. Someone had collapsed from exhaustion. Those immediately close by mistook this for an epileptic fit which was held to be a contagious and dangerous disease. After the trouble had been diagnosed and the unfortunate victim carted away by a team of boy scouts and Local Government policemen, Gorgeous Gregory continued his speech from where it had been interrupted. Moses did not listen to most of what he said. Instead, he busied his mind on many things both relevant and irrelevant to the ceremony. The way Gorgeous Gregory removed, brandished, and replaced his glasses while he spoke, for instance. He had never ceased to be intrigued by this mannerism of Gorgeous Gregory's. He heard vaguely the familiar phrases about the necessity for choosing a worthy chairman to direct the affairs of the occasion, and how those in the Union had looked round and could see no one more able to discharge the onerous duties than their beloved and well-respected Chief Michael Odole, retired Civil Servant and Justice of the Peace, Vice President of the Improvement Union.

The ripple of applause which started at the platform was magnified over the loudspeaker and continued among the crowd long after Chief Odole, his kinsman, had taken the central chair on the platform. Moses rose mechanically with the others when the Chairman invited the vicar of the First Methodist Church to say a prayer for the success of the ceremony. Again, Moses sat down with the others when the man of God had said a long prayer punctuated by several amens. In between he wondered what Dauda would write about the vicar the following day.

'We are already seeing the benefits of the appointment of our Principal as a Minister of State.' The way the Chief said this recalled Moses from his day-dreaming. 'Minister, Minister, Minister. I ask you my people, was it not only the word Minister we heard in the past? How many of us have

B 13

ever seen a Minister in the flesh?' There was a wave of confirmation among the crowd. They had never before that day seen a Minister in the flesh. 'Not only do we now have a Minister in our own town, our own son; but see me now, an old man without education, without a university degree, I am sitting among THREE Ministers of State. Is this not a great thing for us in Newtown? I ask, is it not?'

The crowd cheered the speaker in a very long round of applause. The Minister of Local Government whispered something in Moses' ear. Moses inclined his head slightly to look in the direction indicated by his friend. He smiled non-committally.

'Minister of Works, Minister of Ladies,' his friend again whispered. 'Tell me, who's she?'

Gloria! So Titus Badejo had seen her where she sat. Most probably the signals he had exchanged with her immediately after he had taken his seat had been intercepted by this fellow Titus, and perhaps by a number of others too. He frowned momentarily as he recalled the gossip that had been gathering momentum both in Newtown and Victoria about him and Gloria. He was annoyed that he had spent so much time and energy denying the illicit association between them. The number of lies he had had to tell! God, how one lie necessarily and spontaneously led to another. Now that he was a Minister of State, he wondered if there was anything wrong in having a smart nursing sister as girl friend. He was no longer a schoolmaster. He need no longer abide by the very narrow code of conduct with which the voluntary agency school authorities chained their teachers. It was a short step between thinking of Gloria and dreaming of Gloria from his exposed position on the platform.

Titus Badejo nudged him back to consciousness. 'Wake up, man. It will not do the Party much good if Dauda should put your photograph on the front page of his paper tomorrow. "The sleeping Minister of Works", he would caption it.'

'Thank you.' Moses yawned softly, trying to take his bearing.

'They are about to read the address,' the other Minister said. 'Say, did you have a long session with the lady there last night?'

'Minister, please!' Moses whispered, disgust furrowing his face.

'Oh, you boys with degrees. You pretend you do not do things like that. Yet, you are the most terrible with women – what?'

Moses had pinched him to make him realize that as a Minister of State he was expected to be guarded in word and deed – if not in thought.

'An Illuminated Address Presented by the Newtown Improvement Union on behalf of the Chiefs and the People of the Newtown District Council Area to the Honourable Alade Moses, M.P., B.A. (Hons.), Dip.Ed., Minister of Works in the Government of Afromacoland.'

Gorgeous Gregory read the letters after the name with great emphasis. He paused for the effect that he knew would be forthcoming at the end. It was tremendous. It started from the platform and spread throughout the crowd. Titus Badejo smiled congratulations to his colleague. So did the other Minister, Charles Anjorin, Minister of Education. 'Just how one single man can combine all these degrees and qualifications I don't know,' this latter said to Chief Odole, an observation which was picked up by the table microphone and magnified over the loudspeaker to the delight and amusement of the whole crowd.

'Our dearly respected Minister, our beloved son and fearless nationalist, we the undersigned on behalf of ourselves, the Chiefs and the entire Newtown Community both at home and abroad welcome you today to the town of your birth the status of which you have raised to the level of a first-class city by your recent appointment as a Minister of State in the Government of our beloved country, Afromacoland.' It was obviously all stage-managed. During all these distractions for the crowd, Moses again allowed his own thoughts to wander far away from the proceedings. He thought of many things: of his wife, Bose; of Gloria – oh Gloria. Of the things the Director of Public Works had told him that morning about consulting engineers.

He was recalled to the present by what he heard Gorgeous Gregory saying about him.

'Permit us to say that while you were not born with a silver spoon in your mouth you were born with a golden spoon well tucked away in your family history. For you were born to our dearly respected Elder the late Pa Joshua Alade of the royal family of Aponbepore.'

So Gorgeous Gregory has got it in! His paternal aunt had told him the day before that some important people had been coming to her to ask her to relate to them the history of the family. 'They wanted to know who was the father of your father. They wanted to know who was his own father. I asked them how they expected me to know all these things since I was myself not born at the time. But I told them all that I know. I know that my father's father fought in the Kiriji War and helped to drive the Oyos back. I told them that. And I told them that my father's grandfather was the Chief of Agbado. He was a prince. Only the sons of Obas were made Chiefs in Agbado and the other sixteen towns in the District.' So Gorgeous Gregory had worked on this line and developed his royal descent from Aponbepore. Yes, he'd heard his paternal great aunt greet him 'Son of Aponbepore, Lord of all Agbado' when he was a child.

'We have it on record that you attended St. Paul's School, Newtown, where you set such a record of high scholarship leading to three promotions in one single year and another

16

double promotion two years after as a result of which – [applause] – as a result of which – [more applause still] – as a result of which you finished in five years an elementary school course which others normally take eight full years to complete [prolonged applause]. No other scholar has come near let alone beaten this wonderful, this most enviable scholastic record which you set in our premier elementary school in Newtown seventeen years ago . . .

'You were not blessed with the opportunity of having formal secondary education in a grammar school or in a college. Yet as a pupil teacher in your Alma Mater and by self effort aided by correspondence courses you were able to sit and pass the General Certificate of Education in the First Division in the short space of only four years after you left the elementary school. Others doing full-time attendance in secondary schools take six years or more to pass the same examination in the Second Division. Such a scholastic achievement has never been paralleled in the history of education in this or in any other district in Afromacoland.'

During the applause that followed, Titus Badejo whispered another rude remark to him whereupon both of them laughed. Chief Odole, Moses noticed, was already indulging in a quiet sleep, an embarrassing thing in the exposed position in which he had been placed.

'We as a community are very proud to have seized the opportunity five years ago of awarding you a scholarship to study for a degree in the United Kingdom. We are proud rather because you have, by your wonderful record of passing the B.A. (Hons.) degree in three and the Dip.Ed. in a single year placed the name of our dear town Newtown on the map in the very heart of the British Commonwealth of Nations.'

The burst of applause brought Chief Odole round. He looked from Alade Moses on his left to Titus Badejo on his right. He appeared lost, but only temporarily. He too joined in the applause – quite obviously something had been said that called for this.

'The masterly way in which you steered the ship of our beloved Grammar School for the one and a half years in which you were Principal was a masterpiece of administration and institutional discipline. In that short space of time the name of the school rose at a phenomenal speed both in scholastic achievement, athletic prowess and discipline and morale. "Who is this new Principal of Newtown Grammar School that has raised its standard so high?" was the question on the lips of everyone both in the Secretariat in Victoria and here in Newtown . . .

'We know we need you here in Newtown to continue to guide the fortunes of our Grammar School. But it soon became obvious that academic achievements and intellectual stature mark you out for service at the national level. That is why we reluctantly release you in this community that you may serve our community and the nation at large in the higher capacity of Minister of Works in the Government of Afromacoland.'

Gorgeous Gregory continued after the applause: 'Our fathers say that a little boy that knows how to wash his hands properly will dine with his elders. It is also written in the scriptures: "Seest thou a man diligent in his work? He shall stand before kings and not before commoners." Our dear Minister, son and co-patriot, you have by your great intellectual achievements today brought yourself to a position where you dine with your elders and stand before kings. We have no doubt in our mind whatsoever that you will acquit yourself most creditably in this exalted position to which you have now been called to serve the nation.'

There was some rumbling behind the clouds. But Gorgeous Gregory continued reading the address. 'Behind every great man there is a great woman,' Moses frowned.

'Behind Abraham there was Sarah. Behind Isaac there was Rebecca. And behind our beloved guest of honour of today there is his indefatigable, amiable consort, Mrs Hannah Bosede Moses —' Moses wondered why Gorgeous Gregory had to bring in this portion about his wife. Everyone that had eyes to see knew that Bose was not beautiful and that she was not a wife that the headmaster of a grammar school would be encouraged to introduce to his friends. It was obvious that she was going to become an even greater embarrassment to him now that he had become a Minister. He had married her when both of them were pupil teachers in the Newtown School. She had no parents to object to him on the ground of his obscure family background, as Lola's people had done before he settled on Bose. In the five years in which he studied and improved himself academically before going to University, Bose settled down to the wifely duties of cooking the family meals, producing babies – three girls in five years – and getting fat. When he came back from his oversea studies she was waiting for him, still fatter than when he left her four years before. The gap between their outlooks had grown correspondingly wider. In the nineteen months that he had been back she had produced a set of twin girls and was now expecting another baby, which made her too ill to come to the function.

Moses listened to the concluding portion of the address, the important bit requesting him to use his influence in the Government to bring all modern amenities to Newtown and district: pipe-borne water, electricity, the tarring of the township and district roads, the siting of industries in the town that the exodus of young men from the town and district to Victoria might be arrested. Finally, the address concluded by wishing the new Minister and the new Government success and long life in the service of the nation, and requesting him to accept 'this little gift as a token of our appreciation of all that you have done for the advancement of education and the general progress of our own dear Newtown'.

While Gorgeous Gregory read out importantly the names and the titles that the nine signatories to this important document held in the Newtown Improvement Union, Moses noticed that it was Lola who had been chosen to make the presentation to him. He had seen her a number of times since she returned from the United States where she had done a Bachelor's degree in some subject the evaluation of which had led to muddle and finally complete stalemate between the Ministry of Education, the Ministry of Establishment and the Office of the Prime Minister. Too many officials and influential politicians were known to be interested in Lola's case.

Three

---◇---

SEVEN weeks after his appointment as a Minister, Alade Moses attended an important meeting in the spacious office of the Attorney General and Minister of Agriculture.

The chain-smoking Minister explained to the meeting of five that he had called them together on the instruction of the Prime Minister. He told them that the Prime Minister had charged the Committee with responsibility for giving impetus to, and co-ordinating the activities of, the various Ministries and Departments responsible for the Government's Five Year Development Programme. The Hon. Franco-John was a powerfully built man, a lifelong friend and associate of the Prime Minister since their student days in Britain. There was no official post of Deputy Prime Minister but all in the Party accepted him as the heir-apparent to the leadership. 'We are all familiar with the Party manifesto,' he said. 'We have a heavy programme to go through in our first five-year term of office.' He crushed the remains of a cigarette in the ash-tray.

'An excellent idea,' the Minister of Education said. Charles Anjorin was a fat, elderly man with stained teeth. 'We must show our people that we mean business. We must,' he said, appealing to his colleagues for support.

'But, Chief, we must be businesslike in the way we conduct our business, if we truly mean business,' the Minister of Local Government said sagely. He was the only one of them wearing Western clothes. He was also the youngest.

'Perhaps the "businessman" Minister will explain?' the host Minister suggested. They all chuckled. Then the Minister of Local Government explained: 'If this is a properly called meeting of a Committee of the Cabinet, we must have a proper record of the proceedings. Someone to take the minutes. That would be businesslike,' the young Minister said, pleased with himself.

'Someone to take the minutes,' the Minister of Works muttered to himself. 'A confidential secretary. One that can do shorthand – and keep secrets!'

'And one that has good looks too,' the Minister of Local Government added, quite elated. 'Some of the girls in these offices are smashers. These heads of department certainly know how to take care of themselves.'

'Ministers, please,' Town Planning said, feigning seriousness. 'We are here to discuss the nation's development programme, not girls, beautiful or otherwise. When the electorate voted you in, they did not mandate you to go and look for beautiful girls.' He was short and fat, hiding his poor educational background behind a briar pipe which he continuously smoked.

'Chief of Ladies,' the Minister of Local Government cried, and they all joined in the joke. Like Charles Anjorin the Minister of Town Planning too was notorious for his activities with women.

'Now, gentlemen,' the Attorney General banged the table to bring the meeting nearer to the subject of planning and development, more worthy of the consideration of a committee of Cabinet Ministers. 'Now let's see what the Minister of Works has for us. Your Ministry, I take it, has started on the construction of the new Parliament buildings?'

'But before we start on the main item of discussion, may

I crave the indulgence of the Chairman to bring an important matter to the notice of this meeting?' the Minister of Local Government asked. His colleagues noticed that he was less flippant than he used to be.

'Yes, Minister?' Franco-John encouraged him to proceed.

'It is the question of furniture in the offices of Ministers.,

'Good, good,' the Minister of Town Planning said, beating the table in his jubilation over the introduction of the topic. 'I had meant to introduce the matter myself,' he said, looking round his colleagues in sheer delight.

'The furniture in my office is most disgraceful; I've been begging the Ministry of Works for a replacement for weeks. Not that I'm jealous of the furniture in this room,' Local Government indicated the formica top of the oval table round which they sat, and the equally modern chairs and bookcases in the room. 'I think that something really ought to be done to —'

'I can assure the Minister that a paper is coming before Council soon. It will authorize the issue to each Minister both in his office and in his house furniture befitting the dignity of the high office of a Minister of State.'

'Hear, hear!' The Minister of Town Planning cheered the statement from the host Minister.

'The Minister of Works is responsible for this. Meanwhile, gentlemen, I suggest we now listen to the Minister of Works in connection with the construction of the new Parliament Building. Mr Moses?'

They all looked at Moses. 'We have not yet started on the construction, I fear,' Moses said slowly, aware of the battle that awaited him.

'You have not!' Franco-John remarked, somewhat disappointed. 'How's that? Remember P.M. said that we will hold the next budget session of the House in the new building.' He lit another cigarette, his third since the meeting began.

'I fear that will be impossible,' Moses said slowly as he sorted out a file marked 'SECRET' from a pile which he emptied from his brief-case.

'Impossible, Minister?'

'Absolutely impossible, sir,' Moses said, more deliberately this time, as he flicked through the pages of the file. 'I have had a long discussion with the experts in my Ministry. Experience has taught us to steer clear of rush programmes. I am to advise Government of the need for adequate investigations, designing, and the other important and necessary stages of pre-planning before we actually embark upon the construction of any work project.' He said this with the inward satisfaction of one who has taken in a reasonable fraction of the technical vocabulary on which his Ministry officials had previously briefed him.

They all listened to him with interest and attention, a number of them however, with an obvious lack of understanding of the things he said.

'Parliament building won't be ready before April next year? Somebody is going to be in trouble with P.M.,' Local Government said suggesting in advance something of the wrath sure to descend upon Works when the Prime Minister became aware of the delay.

'Here is the report,' Moses said, taking a few steps from his seat to show the Attorney General and Minister of Agriculture his authority. Chief the Hon. Franco-John glanced through the minute before reading it out.

'Who wrote this?' he asked.

'My Permanent Secretary.'

'"Honourable Minister of Works,"' Franco-John read out to his colleagues. '"The Director of Public Works and I have discussed in detail the proposed Parliament Building project. The Chief Architect's preliminary investigation has revealed some doubt about the capacity of the soil at the proposed site to carry the weight of the type of structure which I understand the P.M. has in mind. It is necessary to do extensive soil tests on the site. After this the most suitable design for the site will be made. After the design we would invite competitive tendering to ensure that the actual work of construction goes to the most suitable contractor in the field."'

'I can tell the most suitable contractor in the field,' Local Government interrupted. 'But go on first, Minister.'

'"The building of a Parliament House in Africa needs very careful handling. We must be careful to ensure that we take all necessary steps that will result in the erection of a building which will remain a lasting monument worthy of this great nation. It is for this reason that the work of planning and designing such a building must be entrusted to consultants of international reputation. The Architects Division of our Ministry is doing excellent work but it is completely inadequate to the handling of a project of this magnitude by itself . . ."'

'Ministry of Works!' someone interrupted.

'You mean Ministry of Waste,' Education derided.

'Who is that Permanent Secretary. Isn't he expatriate?' Local Government asked, visibly annoyed.

'Expatriate, of course. They all are. No black man is good enough to be Permanent Secretary yet,' Town Planning joined in.

'The man's writing must be very good if Chief can read it so well,' Education observed. 'White men don't usually write well. I don't think they learn writing at school.'

'It is typed, not written,' Moses enlightened them.

'"Finally",' Attorney General and Agriculture started on the concluding portion of the minute. Then the telephone rang. 'Ye–e–e–s!' the Honourable Franco-John drawled the word into the receiver. 'Who? Wants to see me? Constituency man? I've told you what to tell people when I'm busy having an important meeting. Look, Mr Man, I'm going to report you to the Secretary to the Prime Minister. Not only will I ask for a new Private Secretary I shall ask that your appointment should be terminated. You beg me, you say? You should beg yourself. Right. Foolish man,' he said, after banging the receiver. 'They want to be in positions of responsibility. When you help them get there, what do they do?' he asked looking round the faces of his colleagues. He mopped his brow with a clean handkerchief and lit another cigarette.

'You were reading the concluding portion of the minute,' Moses helped his senior colleague to regain his bearing.

'I don't think we need to waste any more time over . . .'

'But that last paragraph is the most important part of the minute,' Moses explained. 'Please read it, sir,'

'Let's see now – yes. "Finally, all the steps analysed here will take time. The soil investigations, the selection of the most suitable consultant, the preparation of the drawings and of the contract documents advertising for tenders, the selection of the best tender – all this pre-construction work will take time. So will the actual construction. D.P.W.'s estimate is twenty-four months . . .""'

'Nonsense, absolute nonsense,' cried Local Government.

'Twenty four months!' Attorney General and Agriculture looked up from the paper and searched the face of Moses.

'You see, I called in both the Permanent Secretary and the Director for further explanation . . .'

'Both expatriates, not so?' Local Government forestalled the explanation of his colleague.

'Yes. Both of them,' Alade Moses confirmed.

'And what further explanation did you get?' Attorney-General and Agriculture asked in a tired voice.

'Well, the Director emphasized the importance of the soil investigations. After these investigations, the Consultant will have to prepare many drawings. Very many. The contract documents are actually big books – and there are many copies of them.'

'They are called specifications,' Home Affairs enlightened his colleagues.

'Yes, they are called Specifications and Bills of Quantities,' Moses continued. 'In fact we have to engage another lot of consultants called quantity surveyors for preparing this Bill of Quantities. I went into this in detail. What is disturbing about this Bill of Quantities apart from its cost is that the quantity surveyor cannot start preparing it till the Consultant Architect has finished the drawings. And the surveyor will take about three months to prepare the Bill.'

'Tell me now,' Education implored, 'you mean all this time the contractor cannot start building before the drawings are completed and the surveyor surveys the plan?'

'That's correct,' Moses said expertly. 'You see the contractor requires both the drawings and the Bill of Quantities for building the house.'

'I do not know what you others think,' Town Planning observed producing from the depths of his big damask agbada a big kolanut which he split in two. 'I see here clear evidence of sabotage. Plain as A.B.C.' After a subdivision of one of the halves of the kolanut, he bit off a good slice of one of the quarters and proceeded to chew it noisily.

'Gentlemen, what do you think of this matter?' Franco-John asked his colleagues. The ash-tray on the formica top desk was already full of cigarette-ends. 'This is a very serious matter. What should we do?' he asked yawning.

'What do we do? Simple,' Local Government declared. 'The two expatriate officials in the Ministry of Works are definitely sabotaging Government's effort. Quite clearly they do not want to see the whole thing materialize. The answer is obvious. They must go.'

'The earlier the better,' Town Planning supported his ministerial colleague.

27

When later that day Chief Franco-John discussed the result of the meeting with the Prime Minister, the Secretary to the Cabinet explained the difficulty in the way of removing the expatriate officials in question. There was an understanding with the British Commonwealth Office in London which guaranteed the security of employment for British nationals in the former Colonial Service. He advised that the Director of Public Works should be invited to a meeting with the Prime Minister. Hearing the facts from the horse's mouth would be useful.

Franco-John rang late that night to let Moses know of the decision to have a meeting of his professional adviser in the Ministry with the Prime Minister on the question of the execution of development projects. After the telephone conversation, Moses reflected on the meeting of the Ministerial Committee earlier in the day. It was the first time he had attended such a meeting; he understood one meeting of this kind had been held before he arrived back from his visit to Britain. What struck him most about the meeting was the apparent levity with which his colleagues treated what appeared to him to be important matters. He wondered how Ministers of State spent so much time talking about their mistresses while serious problems of development and administration stared the nation in the face. He had himself taken little part in this side talk about women. If his association with Gloria disqualified him from being an angel, he at least knew how not to contaminate serious matters of state with irreverent gossip about girl-friends.

Four

———————◇———————

THREE days after this, Chief the Honourable Franco-John called on Moses in his office.

'I thought you were having a meeting with the delegation from Jordarmenia,' Moses said as he rose to receive his august visitor. 'According to this programme from the Secretary to the Premier, they should be with you now.'

'Delegation, delegation, delegation – I'm tired of delegations. I'm sick and tired of them,' Chief the Honourable Olagoke Franco-John, Attorney General and Minister of Agriculture, said, seeking the ash-tray as he sank into one of the heavy cushioned chairs. 'Today, it is a delegation from Canada. Tomorrow, it is a delegation from Japan. And the day after, it will be a delegation from the moon . . .'

'Don't think it is impossible Minister,' Alade Moses said, offering his visitor a packet of cigarettes. 'The Russians are already putting the finishing touches to their arrangements for landing on the moon. I'm sure they'll beat the Americans to it.'

'Good thing too. The Americans talk much. They do little. But look at the Russians. They never say a word till they have actually done a thing.' After a deep and rather loud yawn in which his eyes roved round the room, Franco-John said: 'What a palace of an office you have here, Minister. See the chairs, see the desk – why this is better than the mirror in my dressing-room,' he cried admiring his image in the polished top of the desk. 'Why, and the curtains on the windows and the door.' He looked at the carpet which covered the entire floor area of the room. He shook his head and looked at his host inquiringly. 'And you joined the others the other day in the fight for better furniture, Mr Minister?'

'The carpet was from Kingsway Stores. I think it is quite beautiful.' Moses said the obvious, a little embarrassed at the critical eye with which the senior minister took in the details of the furnishing of his room.

Franco-John nodded his head thrice. He crushed the end of his second cigarette in the ash-tray and said: 'I see, it is a case of those who labour at the altar. They shall live upon the altar. Now, Minister' he said, apparently entering upon an entirely different subject. 'What are you doing for our friend in your Ministry?'

Moses looked at his companion with eyes that asked for further clarification.

'Niger Enterprises Ltd.'

'Niger Enterprises Ltd?'

'Yes. You know they've tendered for the State School job. You know the Managing Director is a good Party man. Apart from that, he's good. He is a sport. He's been like that since we were at school together.'

'I see,' Moses said reflectively as he sorted out a green-edged business card from the litter of cards and other papers on his desk. 'Niger Enterprises Ltd,' he read out slowly. 'Leading Firm of Indigenous Contractors. Managing Director: Chief Geo Abyssinia.' After fiddling with the card for some time he said: 'But, Minister, I think I know Abyssinia.'

'You do? Good.'

'He is one of the applicants for the post of Principal of Newtown Grammar School.'

'Of course he is,' the other said with a nod of his head, a little surprised at the revelation.

'Since when did he become a contractor? And who installed him a chief anyway? How can he do the school work well when he is running a contract business?'

'I leave that to you, Minister. Look my duty is to introduce him, which I have done. How he runs the school and his contract business is his look-out. But we need to encourage a man like him in the contracting industry.'

The telephone rang. 'Yes. Yes. Who? The Attorney General? Yes, he's here with me. Who wants him? Who? Yes? He's here. You want him to call to see you after he leaves me? You want to know when you can see him in his office? Let me ask him.' He covered the mouth of the receiver with his right hand as he addressed Franco-John. 'It's the Minister of Education. He wants to know when you will be back in your office.'

'He's having trouble with his constituency again. The people are a nuisance,' Franco-John commented, tapping the end of a new cigarette on his silver case.

'What should I tell him? Do you want to speak to him?'

'No. Not at all. Tell him I'll ring him when I get back in my office.'

'He'll ring you when he gets back in his office,' Moses said to the receiver.

'When?' He repeated into the receiver what must have been a question from the other end.

'Tell him thirty minutes,' Franco-John whispered.

'Half an hour from now. Yes, thirty minutes. What? Yes? The *Afromacoland Sentinel*? Yes. I saw it. Which page? No, I didn't read it.'

'That's the other thing I want to discuss with you, Minister,' Franco-John said as he brought out a newspaper cutting from his diary.

'You've discussed it with A.G.?' Moses again spoke to the phone.

'Yes, he has,' Franco-John said sticking the cutting under the nose of his host. 'And the P.M. has discussed it with me too. A clear case of libel,' Franco-John continued as Moses glanced through the article. He ignored what the voice at the other end of the telephone was saying. He absent-mindedly handed the telephone receiver to Franco-John who continued the conversation with the caller at the other end while Moses read the article:

'The wrath of the God of Africa will descend upon them, the perpetrators of this monstrous crime against the electorate of the nation. And Nemesis will come to all the organs and institutions of society that have aided and abetted the crime. All of them that have made a complete mockery of the sacred institution of the ballot box, all of them that stood in the way of the people's exercising their inalienable right to choose who shall speak for them in the nation's assembly – all of them will pay the penalty at the appointed time.

'We have the greatest admiration for the academic achievements of Alade Moses, the gentleman who was declared returned unopposed in the Newtown North constituency. We know that he knows, more than any of us, that he has not been elected into the nation's legislature in accordance with the electoral regulations. We know him to be a gentleman, a perfect gentleman. And we expect him to behave like a gentleman, a perfect gentleman. And like a gentleman, a perfect gentleman, let him this day, this hour, send to the Prime Minister his letter of resignation as a Minister of State, and to the Clerk of the House of Representatives his letter of resignation as a member of an honourable body to which he has not been properly elected.

'And if he refuses to take an honourable way out in this matter then he should be prepared for battle, real battle. We shall fight him, together with the imperialists and that fascist organization that goes by the name of Newtown Improvement Union. They think that they can direct the wishes and actions of Newtown people by remote control from here in Victoria. Let all of them band together. We shall fight them all. We shall fight them in Newtown. We shall fight them in Victoria. We shall fight them in the highest court of law in the land. We shall fight them till we finish them. We shall fight, we shall never surrender.'

'It's that wretch Dauda again,' Franco-John commented, when he noticed that Alade Moses had finished reading the offending article. He had himself finished his telephone conversation and had for the last minute been watching the frown on Moses' face as he scanned the newspaper cutting line by line. 'I think he's had it this time. He will not get away with it.' Moses looked up at his colleague inquiringly. Then he sighed. 'P.M. himself has seen this article,' Franco-John said.

'He has?'

'Yes, he has,' Franco-John continued. 'And the Party lawyers are already busy studying it. I'm sure this is a clear case of libel.'

Moses nodded his head absent-mindedly. He stared through his companion who continued: 'This is not an attack on an individual. It is an attack on the whole Party. That's what Dauda didn't understand. An attack on one member is an attack on all. And we are going to give him more trouble than he can take personally. And you know what, Minister?'

'Yes?'

'This is criminal libel. I should know what I'm talking about. Libel on a Minister of State in his official capacity is a crime against the State.'

'Criminal libel,' Moses pondered, still looking worried. It was obvious the newspaper article had upset him.

After a short pause during which Franco-John performed the funeral ceremony of one cigarette and the naming ceremony of its successor, he said: 'On second thoughts, I think we should not make it a case of criminal libel against Dauda. Not that we may lose the case. Not at all. If we win the case Dauda will either go to gaol or be made to pay a heavy fine. If he goes to gaol, apart from his being rendered ineffective politically for some nine months, he will become a liability on the State. If he is fined what he pays goes into State revenue. This is no advantage to us. Private proceedings for libel against Dauda. That's what we must arrange. "Alade Moses sues Abdul Dauda for Libel." No, better still: "Alade Moses sues for Libel: Abdul Dauda in court for £100,000 damages claim." Yes, £100,000.'

'£100,000!'

'We ask for £100,000. We'll probably get £15,000, depending on who the judge is, and who our lawyer is.'

'Our lawyer! Who pays his expenses?' Moses asked, alarmed.

'You are not to worry about that. The Party will take care of that. The Party lawyers will handle the preliminaries. That's what they are paid for. But the real case will obviously require a Q.C.'

'That must be very expensive. And the Party's funds can stand this?'

'I know our Party funds are low, very low. People are not paying their subscriptions regularly. The Ministers and Parliamentary Secretaries are not setting a good example at all.'

'I suppose people find it difficult to part with 10 per cent

34

of their salaries,' Moses chuckled. '£15 off one's salary every month is much, you know.'

'The Assembly men who don't hold ministerial appointments are paying their dues fairly regularly, I'm told. And the fellows in the towns and villages are doing fairly well. I believe something like £130 came in last month.'

'£130. I suppose it depends on what we spent in the same month.'

'Exactly. £130 is chicken feed in the scale of Party expenditure. Our Party must think in terms of tens and hundreds of thousands of pounds. £13,000. £130,000. That's more like it. We must improve the machinery for collecting the monthly subscriptions from the Ministers and the Honourable Members and from the Party supporters from all the constituencies. But clearly, we must look for other sources for the bulk of our finances.'

'Well, the libel case,' Moses said smiling.

'Exactly. And it is more important than you may think. The Party finances the expenses of the Alade Moses *versus* Abdul Dauda libel suit. Pays sixty guineas to the Q.C. Wins £15,000. Pays another forty guineas after to the Q.C.'

'A hundred guineas to the lawyer then.'

'In fact we will require the personal intervention of P.M. before the Queen's Counsel will take a hundred guineas. Two hundred. Three hundred. That's what he charges for big cases. In any case you pay him a hundred or two hundred guineas. The Party lawyers another two hundred for their own labours.'

'Yes?'

'And of course you, Minister. We mustn't forget to pay the victim of the outrageous libel. One hundred, two hundred? No, we make it five hundred guineas. After all, your character has been assassinated by Dauda. It all still leaves the Party with a lot more money than we can ever hope to raise from monthly subscriptions.'

'I see.'

'And, Minister. You should remember to look into the case of Niger Enterprises Ltd.,' Franco-John said as he was rising to go out. 'Geo Abyssinia is a sport, Minister. We need people like him to support us – and the Party.'

After Franco-John had left him Moses reflected for some time on the unpleasant situation developing round him. He had thought that after he had ignored Dauda's first attack on him in the *Afromacoland Sentinel* the opposition leader had left him alone and that the question of the alleged irregularity in the manner of his election had been forgotten. To his great disappointment and annoyance, this new publication now showed that neither was Dauda leaving him alone, nor was the question of the way he entered Parliament being forgotten.

Now Franco-John wanted him to use his position as Minister of State to get Geo Abyssinia contracts in his Ministry. Apart from his own personal abhorrence of corruption, he knew that to do this was to give Dauda a second rope with which to double the noose round his neck. And from what he now knew of Dauda, he was not one for missing opportunities.

Geo Abyssinia, Managing Director of Niger Enterprises! Moses recollected that he had known him as a clubman. He played billiards hour after hour, and Moses had wondered when he ever got round to doing whatever work he did for a living. He stood a drink to everyone that came in. He himself drank everything that came in alcoholic form, though it did not appear to have on him any of the nuisance effects that alcohol is supposed to have on its addicts.

The night before, Moses and Theo George, the most senior Afromacolese engineer in the Ministry of Works and a former associate of Moses in student politics in Britain, had met and given the Minister a few unofficial tips about the Ministry. This was in the A3 bungalow of a mutual friend, Geoffrey

Shepherd, the expatriate Principal of State College in Victoria. Moses remembered that Theo George had told him of the sinister activities of Chief Abyssinia and his personal disappointment that his boss, the Director of Public Works, and the Permanent Secretary had not handed the rogue over to the police before then.

He shook his head as he remembered the complaints against Theo George himself. Anonymous letters accused him of preferring expatriate contractors to indigenous contractors. One letter actually said that he was a hater of his kind and race, revelling in the downfall and misfortune of Afromacolese contractors. Theo George had explained his own side to Moses. The so-called Afromacolese contractors were no contractors at all. They had no basic training or experience in any of the building trades, no equipment, no stores or yard. They refused to join together to form large viable firms. Yet they insisted on being given work clearly beyond their competence. Moses remembered how George had explained all this with feeling. He wondered what would be the solution to the problem of the African contractor.

Five

THE meeting in which the Director of Public Works was to explain to the Prime Minister the difficulties in the way of implementing the development projects was held in the study in the Prime Minister's Lodge eleven days after the Ministerial Committee meeting at which the sacking of the expatriate Permanent Secretary and Director of Public Works had been recommended as a solution to the problems which Moses had put before the meeting.

John Harrington, Director of Public Works, had parked his old Ford Zephyr neatly in the tarmac park at the other side of the drive in the Prime Minister's Lodge exactly ten minutes before eleven, the time fixed for the meeting. He had allowed himself thirty minutes for the three and a half miles motoring through the heavily congested portion of the trunk A road that led to the Reservation where the Prime Minister and Ministers lived with senior government officials in comfort and sanitation that contrasted very sharply with the slum conditions that prevailed in Victoria proper. Harrington would have arrived seventeen minutes early. But he had deliberately driven into a side street where he could cool off without being noticed by anyone.

Harrington waited not ten but thirty-five minutes in the waiting-room, trying to hide his nervousness behind the wide sheets of the Government-owned newspaper. He pretended to be reading, but in truth he was nauseated by the bad print, the bad English, and the false propaganda.

While Harrington waited, the Prime Minister was having a conference with Franco-John, Moses, and three other Ministers on the wisdom of pursuing the case of libel against Dauda. Apparently the Solicitor General had written a long minute to the Attorney General pointing out technical complications in the case. The case had what appeared to him to be a fifty-fifty chance at best. At worst it might go against the Minister. In any case he said the view that he was expressing was his own personal opinion. He thought it was wise his Department was not handling the case in view of the great shortage of staff. But as usual he awaited further instructions from the Attorney General.

Moses was for dropping the whole matter. He thought it would be bad publicity for himself and for the Government. He had now heard conflicting accounts of what really took place in Newtown while he was away; he had reason to want the whole matter dropped. The Prime Minister said that it was a legal matter and in legal matters he wished to be advised by the lawyers and the Attorney General. Franco-John said that they had a fifty-fifty chance as the Solicitor General had pointed out and like all lawyers he too advised that the case be taken to court. Dauda must be taught a lesson and he must be ruined financially. Apart from this the Party's finances were bad. They needed the damages that Dauda would pay Moses.

That was how the matter was left when the Prime Minister instructed his Principal Private Secretary to call in Mr Harrington. Moses and Franco-John stayed on while the three other Ministers left the room.

'I want you to be at ease, John,' the Prime Minister told the nervous Englishman as he piloted him into one of the chairs at the conference table. 'Be perfectly frank. Tell us the facts. But I warn you we will not necessarily accept your advice.' He offered him a cigar. 'This Government is committed to a programme of development which we must carry out in our first five-year term of office. The whole thing centres round your Ministry. Do I understand you say you are not equal to the task?' The politician searched the face of the Englishman challengingly.

'May I first of all pledge once more the unqualified loyalty of all the professional officers in the Ministry of Works, both expatriate and indigenous, to your Government. In particular, I pledge my personal loyalty and co-operation. I may with your permission say that after twenty-three years' service in Africa, I can now claim that Africa is my country. I am a foreigner in the country of my birth.'

The Prime Minister chuckled and nodded his head understandingly. But Franco-John was not going to commit himself till he knew where the Englishman was leading to. Moses smiled.

'Most of the projects in the Approved Estimates under Head 306: "Capital Works, Ministry of Works", cannot be done this year, sir. They . . .'

'But Mr Harrington, they have to be done this year,' Franco-John said menacingly.

The Englishman continued, nervous. 'Most of the projects have not even been investigated, let alone designed. All engineering projects must be properly investigated and designed before the actual work of construction is begun.'

'So after the design construction can start?' the Prime Minister asked.

'No, sir. After the design the quantity surveyor measures from the drawings the quantities of work to be done. It is these quantities that will be given to tendering contractors to price. It is after the preparation of the bill of quantities and their pricing first by the quantity surveyor and later by the contractors that the actual extent of Government's financial commitment will be known. It is absolutely essential that the actual extent of Government's commitment is known before we embark upon the construction of any project.'

'Tell me something, Mr Harrington,' the Prime Minister said after some pause. Franco-John smoked away his annoyance. Moses was silent. 'Your observations about the need for investigations, designs, and the work of quantity surveyors applies not only to the Parliament Building project, but to all engineering projects?'

'Quite so, sir. Quite so, sir.'

'This means that all the road construction projects, water supplies, electricity – all these must undergo the same procedure, Mr Harrington?'

'I am afraid so, sir. But . . .'

'I see, I see. Mr Harrington,' the Prime Minister said sadly, 'this Government is committed to carry out the projects listed in the Estimates. They are the projection of my Party's Election Manifesto. They must be carried out without fail. I must express my gratitude to you for your candour. Behind the apparently unyielding attitude of the professional engineer in you I can see the Englishman's dogged attachment to perfection. Your countrymen will stick to the perfect solution to any problem. They will wait for centuries for the perfect solution. But ours is a country in a hurry. We are committed in our first five-year term in office to provide more schools and hospitals, roads and bridges, water supplies and electricity schemes – we are committed to build more industries in these five years than the colonial government provided in half a century of colonial rule. You will understand then if and why we may have to look for some other way of carrying out our plans. Mr Harrington, I want you to enter into our feeling and share with us our aspirations. Where there's a will there's a way. As you yourself have admitted, you are already one of us.' That pleased Harrington. He smiled to show it.

After some pause, the Prime Minister addressed Moses: 'Minister, I want you to have further discussions with your officials. I am sure Mr Harrington will now approach the assignment with a different attitude. And by the way, Mr Harrington, how are the Afromacolese engineers in your Ministry shaping up?'

'Excellently well, Prime Minister,' the Englishman answered most readily. 'They are most promising indeed.'

'Good, very good.' The Prime Minister expressed satisfaction. Moses nodded. Franco-John smoked on noncommittally.

'They still of course require plenty of experience to hold responsible positions. Engineering requires wide experience to be built on a foundation of academic qualification. Many years. But these boys are coming on nicely, very nicely.'

'I see, I see,' the Prime Minister muttered. 'Tell me, Mr Harrington, how soon can we have an Afromacolese to become your Deputy?'

'A very difficult question, Mr Prime Minister,' the Englishman laughed in confusion. 'Well, let's put it this way. Theo George is the most senior of the boys now. A most able chap, Theo, an all-rounder. He is now Executive Engineer Grade I. He was elected an Associate Member of the Institution of Civil Engineers last June. I'm personally proud of this achievement. I'm thinking of making him act as Senior Executive Engineer soon. In another four years we might try him on the Chief Engineer's schedule. And after two years in that acting capacity —'

'You mean he will not be ripe to be Deputy Director of Public Works for another six years?' Franco-John cried.

'But you see, Minister —'

'And perhaps another sixty years after that before we have

an Afromacolese Director of Public Works? God Almighty!' Franco-John cried, outraged.

'But Minister —'

'I see, I see,' the Prime Minister interrupted the already confused Englishman, looking first at Franco-John and next at Moses. 'This is a matter that we have to give serious consideration, Ministers. Very serious consideration. Meanwhile, Mr Harrington,' he said warmly to Harrington and offering his hand, 'thank you very much indeed. You will be hearing further from your Minister.'

In bed that night Moses reflected on the toughness of the assignment on his plate. He was glad that the Prime Minister himself had seen the magnitude of the problem he faced in the Ministry of Works, a thing that Franco-John appeared not to see. To him it appeared that Moses had not been firm enough with his officials. Surely there was a limit to which one could be firm with experts in their own field! How he wished he was in the Ministry of Education.

He fell asleep – and dreamt of Gloria.

Six

---◇---

GORGEOUS GREGORY, Secretary General of Newtown Improvement Union, made himself more and more indispensable to Alade Moses. He now styled himself Political Secretary to the Minister of Works. In that capacity he supervised and interfered with the work of the young official Private Secretary posted from the office of the Prime Minister.

He was with the Minister when on a Thursday morning, four months after his appointment, Moses received a delegation from the Union. When the leader of the delegation observed humorously that it was difficult to know on which side of the net Gregory was playing, he explained the need to shuttlecock between the two offices. He had to keep an eye on the Minister's office to see how things were going on in case someone bungled things and exposed Moses, the brightest jewel in Newtown's crown, to ridicule. In spite of this important assignment with the Minister, Gorgeous Gregory was still fully in charge of the Union's headquarters office in Newtown.

There were seven in the delegation, led by their First Vice-President, Chief Michael Odole. They were obviously awed by the first-class furniture and the artificial cold in the room. To have been allowed to enter such an office and sit in the heavily upholstered chairs was a great amenity which the appointment of Moses had brought them. On behalf of himself and the other members of the delegation Chief Odole congratulated Moses yet again on his appointment as Minister of State and thanked him for the glory he had brought to their hometown. He then delved into the history, aims and objects of the Union. A typewritten sheet of these was then presented to Moses by the Assistant Secretary. Moses noticed that Gregory appeared to be taking shorthand notes of the proceedings having told the Private Secretary that he would cover this meeting himself.

The Assistant Secretary glanced through another typewritten sheet and announced that the first item on the agenda was the Principalship of the Newtown Grammar School. He then called on a member to speak on this. The member got up and went through the usual processes of congratulations and wishes of long life for Moses that he might enjoy the fruits of his labour. He then traced the history of the school from its founding to the time when Moses left the school to become a Minister of State. When he left the Union were anxious that his place should be taken by someone of ability and experience, so that the great standard which he had himself set should not fall. After very serious consideration of all the applicants the Board of Governors with the approval of the Union had appointed Chief Geo Abyssinia. And since he assumed duty he had done very well indeed. In particular he had shown that he was a great disciplinarian. They were therefore shocked and disappointed when they heard that the Ministry of Education had refused to approve the appointment of Geo Abyssinia. They had information in Newtown that Dauda and his gang were at the bottom of the whole thing. They had undoubtedly bribed officials of that Ministry and persuaded them to write a letter to the Board of Governors turning down the appointment of Abyssinia. The Union had come to implore

Moses to use his influence with his colleague, the Minister of Education, to instruct his officials not to molest Abyssinia.

Moses was about to reply to this when Gorgeous Gregory took the floor. He went through his usual mannerisms of removing and replacing his glasses on his nose – an audience consisting of a State Minister and seven co-citizens and fellow officers of a tribal union was entitled to a full display. Pompously he emphasized the importance of the matter raised in the delegate's speech. It was also most delicate as it touched on high policy issues to which the Minister was going to give serious consideration. But he required time to give to it this serious consideration.

Suddenly one of the three telephones rang. Gregory tiptoed from the side table to the Minister's desk. 'This is the office of the Minister of Works: Principal Political Secretary speaking,' he said importantly. The delegates looked on admiringly. 'Yes, yes. No. The Minister is very busy at an important conference just now. Yes, yes. You should book an appointment with the Private Secretary. Yes, yes, bye-bye.' When he came back he said, as he was taking his seat, 'You see the sort of thing I've been saying. Everyone wants to see the Minister. Everyone. If we allow them this place will be packed full with all sorts of people.'

'True, very true,' Chief Odole said, nodding his head. 'Thank you very much for all you're doing for him, Mr Gregory.'

'Very true indeed,' Alade Moses confirmed. 'The number of people that insist on seeing me, my God!'

'And the Minister must be sheltered from all such people. Only the important visitors like your delegation must be allowed to come in. You see what I mean?'

The Assistant Secretary rose up to say how they truly appreciated the importance of the Minister's position and how they appreciated the honour he had done them – they

46

would remain eternally grateful. He then called upon another member to speak on the next subject.

The member did. It concerned Theo George, the District Engineer of the Ministry of Works in Newtown. His activities were inimical to the interest of both the community and the Improvement Union. He was unduly harsh to everyone. He was not liked by anyone – in fact all his workers hated him and wanted him removed. It was the wish of the whole of Newtown community that he should be transferred from Newtown.

'But I thought he was doing excellent work, particularly in aiding the communal labour projects,' Moses observed, rather surprised at this allegation and move against George.

'Minister, the man is bad. We don't want him any more, that is all,' the delegate who had stated the case against George said with a finality that indicated no room for further argument on the matter. Moses recalled seeing the man assume this attitude on more than one occasion at meetings of the Board of Governors when he was still Principal of the Grammar School.

After going through the usual preliminaries with his glasses, Gregory declared that the matter of Theo George raised issues of fundamental importance which required the most serious consideration. He assured the delegation that the Minister would give the matter immediate personal attention.

They discussed the third matter in between frequent telephone interruptions. The Union had heard that Moses was planning to leave the Ministry of Works and to transfer to the Ministry of Education. They had given the matter serious thought and decided that he should remain where he was.

Moses wondered how they knew his mind on this matter, so he asked them.

'You want to know how we know? Look, Minister, we

don't have book knowledge,' one of the delegates said. 'And because we have no book knowledge we must develop our own way of reading the minds of those with book knowledge. If we don't we'd all be sold as slaves before we knew where we were.' He laughed heartily at his own worldly philosophy and the others joined in.

'You see I don't say that I'm thinking of going to the Ministry of Education. Nor do I say that I am not going. But for the sake of argument, why shouldn't I work in a Ministry that I like, so long as the Prime Minister does not object?'

'Look, Minister,' the delegate who had talked against Theo George earlier on said. 'We want you to be Minister of Works. We in the Union want our son to be Minister of Works. We told the Prime Minister so. And he agreed with us. He made you Minister of Works. And —'

The telephone rang, mercifully putting an end to the man's speech, which had been rising in pitch.

Moses noticed while he was speaking on the telephone that his visitors put their heads together and whispered vigorously and that Gorgeous Gregory appeared to be very much in their confidence judging by the way he participated in these conversations. On which side was he? – the question the leader of the delegation had jokingly raised earlier on recurred to Moses.

The discussion proceeded, but not from the point where it had been interrupted. Some other members of the delegation at the prompting of the Assistant Secretary, raised the next issue. This turned out to be the naming of streets. Members of the Union had heard from their secret intelligence that Government had decided to call the streets in the new housing layout in Victoria by the names of prominent men and of important towns in the country. They in Newtown had prominent men and their town was very important, so they wanted Moses to be on the alert so that when the exercise was done Newtown would receive the good treatment it deserved.

'Naming of streets – in the new layout?' Moses' face betrayed a depth of ignorance that did not do justice to a Minister of State. 'Who told you of this?'

Gorgeous Gregory came to the rescue. 'The whole question of allocation of plots and of the naming of streets in the new layout is still confidential, very confidential,' he said. 'The Minister is surprised and embarrassed that you have heard about this matter. If his Cabinet colleagues should hear that he has been discussing the matter with you they would think that he has been leaking Cabinet secrets. And that would be a serious thing against him.'

They all looked worried. They did not want anything serious brought against the brightest jewel in Newtown's crown. Moses himself was amazed how easily the improvised answer flowed from Gregory's lips.

'Nevertheless you must know that the Minister knows your wants more than you know them,' Gregory declared.

'Indeed he does,' one of the men muttered, nodding his head.

'It never happens that we have in charge of the orange tree a man from our own clan and yet be doomed to have oranges that are not ripe,' Gregory quoted a famous proverb. 'More than that would commit the Minister – our Minister by the grace of God.'

The day after this meeting with the men from Newtown, Gorgeous Gregory told Moses that Geo Abyssinia had donated twenty guineas to the scholarship fund of the Newtown Improvement Union.

'Geo Abyssinia – twenty guineas!' Moses exclaimed.

'Yes, twenty guineas. And he told me that that is just the first instalment.'

'Really? But he is not a Newtown man,' Moses said,

looking into the face of his companion as if he could read there the meaning of Abyssinia's unexpected philanthropy.

'Ah, that's the point, Minister. Geo Abyssinia is a Newtown man even though he has not been identifying himself with Newtown in the past. One of these Victoria people whose ancestors originally came from the provinces – those whose ancestors were sold to slavery in the West Indies but found their way back to the country through Freetown. Either because they couldn't trace the towns and villages from which their ancestors originally left or because they preferred the more sophisticated life on the coast to the backward standard of living in the interior, they settled down in Victoria.'

'I see, another one of these Victoria Newtownians who really don't know Newtown. I do not think much of them.' Moses pulled a long draught at his beer – they were relaxing in the Minister's private quarters. 'They consider every one of us as a provincial and would have nothing to do with us. It is only when they want some benefit, some favour, that they suddenly discover their Newtown origins. We must beware of Abyssinia, Gorgeous Gregory.'

'Leave that to me, Minister. I've known him for a long time. He is good – a perfect gentleman. And he can really help us with the Union, particularly here in Victoria.'

From the particular case of Geo Abyssinia, Moses and Gorgeous Gregory went at some detail into the harnessing of the potential patriotism of the Victoria Newtownians. Arrangements should be made for attracting them to Newtown. Prominent ones among them should be honoured with chieftaincy titles. Land was to be sold to them on which to build houses that would do Newtown proud.

Two days later Geo Abyssinia again occupied part of Moses' time. At about ten in the morning Franco-John rang up to say that Moses should see him at once in his own office.

Moses hurried to the Ministry of Justice, certain in his mind that something was wrong. The Private Secretary announced him and immediately ushered him in.

Franco-John went straight to business. He told Moses that the Opposition Leader Dauda was up to some pranks. He had organized an election petition against Moses in the High Court. The Prime Minister had been officially informed of this by the Registrar of the Court. Franco-John had been mandated to tell Moses and to work with the Party lawyers to see that Dauda and his gang lost the case.

For some time Moses was speechless. Franco-John crushing the remains of a cigarette in an ash-tray, said: 'Look, Moses, you must expect some hard knocks in politics. I know you cannot be expected to jump for joy at being taken to court. But you must realize that it is all a game. A game of wits. The smartest and the luckiest wins. And to the loser we say, better luck next time.'

'I suppose the Party must be wishing me better luck next time, even now.'

'Why, already giving up, man?'

'Wouldn't you, with all the facts that we know? Are all the allegations about the contravention of the electoral regulations not true? I'm already fed up with the whole thing.'

'Look, as a lawyer I can tell you that we have a very good case. More than a fifty-fifty chance.'

'Yes?'

'Yes. One very important point will win us the case. It is our trump card. Chief Geo Abyssinia has furnished us with the weapon.'

Moses looked at his host inquiringly.

Franco-John continued: 'Dauda did not file the election petition in his own name. He thought he was being clever when he made one of his lieutenants sign the papers. Quite unknown to Dauda this man – I don't remember his name – has served a prison sentence in the North before. Abyssinia was in the North at the time and he has tipped us off. The wretched Dauda is going to have the surprise of his life when the case goes before Mr Justice Kay.'

'How I wish I wasn't the centre of all this,' Moses muttered sadly.

'And by the way, Minister, I hear the libel case is coming up on Wednesday.'

'Yes. I hear so too.'

'The chances are excellent. I think we can congratulate ourselves in advance.'

Knowing little about politics and less about law, Moses thought it wise to be guided by the opinion of Franco-John, a man experienced in the one and learned in the other.

Seven

———————◇———————

ALADE MOSES began to wonder if he had not made a mistake in leaving his job as Principal of Newtown Grammar School to become a Minister of State. This was five days after the visit of the members of the Newtown Improvement Union. He had come back late from the office. He had only pecked at his lunch, a cross between the European dish considered by the cook necessary to dignify the table of a Minister of State and the Afromacolese national dish of fried plantains liberally spiced with pepper.

He instructed the driver to take the car to the garage for a check-up. He told the police orderly and the steward that he would see no one whatsoever. If anyone came or rang, they were to be told that he was not in. Then he wearily mounted the steps full of thought. He lay down on the settee on the top landing, which he had converted into a small, private sitting-room.

Four months before he had not the slightest idea that he would be anywhere other than in the modestly furnished office at the Grammar School. Now he was a Minister of State, meeting and sharing dirty jokes with colleagues most of whom he was meeting for the first time, some of whom he did not like. He was not sure where to place Franco-John.

The one immediate advantage he thought he had seen in leaving the school was freedom from the domination of the members of the Newtown Improvement Union, who really ruled the school. But they had followed him to his Ministry to tell him which portfolio he should keep and which he should not. His Cabinet post was clearly a gift to his constituency, a reward for keeping Dauda out, in spite of what the Prime Minister had told him about his qualifying to be a Minister of State irrespective of what constituency he came from.

To keep Dauda out had meant his people contravening the electoral regulations. Now see where that had landed him – in court with an election petition against him! He had been told not to worry. Dauda would lose the case, thanks to a defect in the qualifications of the petitioner. In any case he did not have to bear the expenses of the court action. As a Minister of State the Solicitor General's Department were conducting his defence.

He wondered why a decision in the libel case had taken so long. He knew that cases dragged on endlessly in the magistrates' courts, but he had once heard that the judicial machine ground much faster in the High Court. Supposing he lost the libel case. That would be too bad – for the Party. And if he lost the election petition case – what would happen to him? He wouldn't be able to go back to the Grammar School. Geo Abyssinia would have been officially installed as Principal.

But would he? Moses had still to see how he could persuade his colleague, the Minister of Education, to set aside the relevant portion of the Education Code which disqualified Abyssinia from being Principal.

Moses was already snoring softly when Gloria arrived. She now came in and went out of his house without any inhibitions. The droning of the engine of her Volks 1200 woke him. He heard her exchange greetings with the police orderly. He noticed that he did not stop her! The absence of the car in the drive no doubt made her think that he had not come back from the office. She tiptoed across the sitting-room to the dining-room and thence to the kitchen.

'Good afternoon, madam,' the cook said, looking up from washing the dishes at the aluminium sink.

'Good afternoon, Patrick,' she said. 'You give Master fine chop?'

'Fine, fine chop, madam. Fine, fine chop. But Minister no eat much. I wan make you tell Minister say make he eat my fine, fine chop. Den me I go glad. And Minister he go big.'

'Good, Patrick,' she laughed. She was on good terms with this cook-steward Patrick. She knew the importance of keeping on the good side of the domestic servants in an establishment where she was not the official mistress. She again tiptoed across the dining-room and then made for the staircase. She picked her steps, doing her best to suppress the ones that creaked.

Moses knew that she had not known that he was in. While she was still in the kitchen he had slipped into the guest-room: he was going to catch her unawares. When he came out of the guest-room and entered the main bedroom stealthily he discovered that she was not there, but the sound of running water indicated that she was in the bathroom. He noticed too that in the brief moment that she was in the bedroom before going into the bathroom she had done some rearranging of things in the room. He sighed reflectively. If only he had been free to choose whom he would live with. If only he had known the future and the higher status awaiting him, then he would not have married the Higher Elementary Pass Bose who was totally unfit for looking after the house and the affairs of a Minister of State. Bose was much too timid to go to public places with him – he was much too ashamed to take her too. After bearing five children she had gone fat and grown careless in her appearance.

'Isn't there something in your parliamentarians' code of conduct that says that you should knock the door before you enter a room?' Gloria said without looking up from some washing she was doing in the wash-hand basin.

'Ah, even though you are in your own house?' Moses protested, closing the door softly behind him.

'Even if it is your wife in the room,' she said, looking at him through the mirror of the shaving cabinet, 'you still have to knock the door.'

'I see you have been tidying up the house,' he said as he noticed that she had restored some order among the towels on the chrome-plated rail. She had wiped the floor too and the whole place looked more worthy of the glazed wall tiles. He shook his head. He was surprised she had done all this in the short time since she came upstairs.

'Say what's on your mind,' she said.

'What's on my mind? You guess.'

'It's you who have something on your mind that will say it – if it's worth hearing.' At that point the telephone rang. He went into the bedroom and lifted the receiver. Patrick was already speaking to the caller from downstairs. 'I say, Minister is not in,' he heard Patrick say emphatically.

'Where is he gone to?' he heard the voice at the other end say.

'Master is not in,' Patrick repeated.

'I say where is he gone to . . . ?

'How I fit know where Minister go. You tink say he tell me where he go? Master is a Minister, sir. He can go which place he like.'

Moses smiled, replacing his receiver softly. Good old Patrick! He was already skilled in the important business of sheltering his master from unwelcome callers.

'Oh for a woman to live with in a house like this,' he

declared as he re-entered the bathroom. He knew this would bring a provocative comment from Gloria.

'Then send for Bose,' she said simply. He noticed that her well-laundered nurse's white uniform was already hanging from the hook on the bathroom door and that she was in her white underskirt. She was at that moment washing the soap off her face and so could not see the desire in his eyes as they fed on the nipples of her breasts which swelled out under the lace and nylon bra.

'Look, Glor, why must you keep on bringing up Bose's name all the time?'

'She's your wife, isn't she?' She took the face towel and massaged her face.

'When you come to me I don't want you to remind me of what I want to forget.' He encircled her waist with his arms. She did not resist.

'If you must bring anyone here you had better bring Bose. Not any of those other girls who are fluttering round you.'

'Who are you talking about?' he said apprehensively. His fingers moved upwards, reaching for her breasts. She did not resist.

'I say who do you have in mind?' he repeated.

'Lola. You know very well.'

'Good Lord, woman. Because you saw Lola with me at the Prime Minister's party you think there's something between me and her? Good Lord.'

'There *was* something between you and her. But know that whatever there is between you and her does not worry me. Nevertheless beware. That girl believes in juju. And...'

'But do you, a nursing sister, believe in juju?' He released her, wheeled her round to look her full in the face.

'Look, Alade, you have got to be very careful about Lola, and about girls like her. And I am very serious about it.' She began to remove her frock from the hook. She certainly looked serious as she led the way into the bedroom.

57

'Look, Glor, why won't you take my explanation about Lola – just why?' he asked anxiously.

'You really want to know why?' she said, sitting at the edge of the bed in a way that warned him that she was not going to have any love-making till they had disposed of this matter.

'Of course, I do. I've told you the whole story of our association in the past. But all that is past history now. I'm finished with her —'

'That's just the point. Is she finished with you?'

'Is she finished with me?' he repeated the question after her, looking truly puzzled.

'Yes, is she finished with you?'

'I imagine she is. In any case, I dictate the pace now, not she – nor her wealthy father. Not even if he rises from the grave.'

She looked at him and shook her little head, as if in pity for his ignorance. 'You may know education, you may know politics. But you know what you don't know? Women. You hear, Minister of State, B.A. Dip.Ed., you hear?'

'Yes?'

'You don't know women. I am a woman, and I know what I'm talking about. In your own interest and for your own safety, keep Lola and girls like her at arms' length. I'm dead serious about it.'

Her smile contradicted her protestation of seriousness. She was already thawing, but he knew that he must be careful not to rush her. To his greatest surprise she wanted to know if he had seen the Minister of Education about her uncle Geo Abyssinia.

'Your uncle?'

'Yes. He's my uncle. I too did not know it till last week,' she said, still trying to keep him at bay. 'Apparently he and my father are second cousins. Some big quarrel over family land had stood between the two sides of the family long before I was born. Important people in the village are meeting to settle the quarrel.'

'I see,' he sighed. What he saw was more than Gloria's explanation. It was the fact that Abyssinia was already exploiting his association with her to his advantage. He wondered how she could warn him against girls like Lola while she was herself at that moment going to use her influence with him to advance the interest of her kinsman whom she erroneously called her uncle.

Before she left late in the evening she warned him about the need to do something about the case in court. It was not enough to take Franco-John's assurances. Contact must be made with the judge. As for the election petition case she agreed with him that the matter be left as it was at that time, lest publicity make Dauda discover and rectify the defect in their case.

Eight

———————◇———————

AFTER his driver had manœuvred his Opel Kapitan to a stop on the tarmac outside the Ministry of Education, Moses took out the envelope from his breast pocket. He took out the letter and stayed a few moments in the car to read it again. It was signed by some official for the Director of Education. It revoked the approval given twenty-six months before for the top form of Newtown Grammar School to sit the School Certificate examination till the school was in a position to satisfy the requirements of Section 137 of the Education Code. There were two attachments: a copy of the relevant portion of the Education Code, and a Ministry of Education circular which made a slight amendment to the original Regulation.

As Moses climbed out of the car through the door which the driver held open for him he recollected the meeting which he had had with the delegation from the Newtown Improvement Union. They wanted Geo Abyssinia to be Principal and left Moses to sort out whatever difficulties there were in the way. He also remembered the love scene in his bedroom the day before, when Gloria had disclosed her interest in the Abyssinia case.

Once more he was worried about the propriety of what he was going to ask his Cabinet colleague to do. He thought he knew what was right and what was wrong. But he also knew that since he became a Minister of State a good many things had been done by his colleagues which were not right. Sometimes done by the Cabinet collectively; most often done by individual ministers. He saw nothing wrong in putting the matter before Charles Anjorin. It would then become a matter between the Minister and his Ministry officials.

The Private Secretary asked the crowd of people in the waiting-room to make way for him. He went through the door which the young Civil Servant had opened for him.

'The great Minister of Works – Minister of Ministers,' Charles Anjorin said, offering him his fat hand.

'You know who's waiting for you, Minister?' he said in a low voice to his host as he made sure that the door was closed behind him. 'A very beautiful lady. I think I've seen her before – I just can't remember the exact place.'

'Oh, that's Mrs – er – I've forgotten which Mrs she calls herself now. Her husband is studying accountancy in England, she says. I think the man is stranded there, my brother,' Anjorin said, setting off the knuckles of his plump fingers in a series of explosions.

'Stranded, eh?'

'Yes. And she wants to go and meet him in England.'

'And she wants to take you along with her, Minister?'

Anjorin laughed merrily.

'If a girl like that comes my way I'm sure I'd follow her to the ends of the earth,' Moses declared.

Again Anjorin laughed boisterously, the expanse of his belly visible through the folds of his gaberdine agbada going up and down like the bellows at the blacksmith's. Then he said, still laughing: 'But my Ministry officials are not co-operating. They don't seem to like her.'

'They don't?'

'She wants a scholarship. They say she is not qualified.'

61

'I see,' Moses said.

'She doesn't have the G.C.E. And they want her to get some other qualification. These people, they confuse me in this place,' and he laughed noisily again.

'I see, I see. But Minister, why not give her a scholarship of your own. And give her something else in addition,' Moses laughed mischievously.

'But my brother, one must be careful in this place,' Anjorin confided. 'One will be in real trouble if one is not careful. I never knew there were so many beautiful girls in Victoria till I became Minister of Education. Nursing sisters, women traders, party supporters —'

'And women education officers,' Moses said, accepting a cigarette from Anjorin.

'Yes, women education officers,' Anjorin said more seriously. 'But Minister, you know that they are the bones that are strung into the collar round the neck of a dog.'

'Yes?'

'The dog is forbidden to touch such bones. Yes? Who?' Anjorin was now attending to a buzz on his intercom. 'No, you must tell her that I'm busy with the Minister of Works now. She can ring again in another fifteen minutes. Yes. Another one,' he nodded to Moses after replacing the receiver of the intercom.

'Minister of ladies!' Moses said in mischievous admiration.

'You see my trouble,' Anjorin said, obviously enjoying the reputation.

Moses explained his problem, to which Anjorin listened indifferently, which nearly upset Moses beyond recovery. Anjorin then confessed that he did not see why the proprietors of the Grammar School should not have a principal of their choice. But he did not want to appear to be taking decisions above the head of his Ministry officials. So he buzzed the Director of Education.

After a few moments there was a knock at the door and

Derek McDonald came in. When he saw that his Minister was not alone he said apologetically, 'I beg your pardon, sir,' and he withdrew, closing the door after him.

'Come in, D.E., come in,' Anjorin said, laughing. 'These people with their hypocrisy. Why is he running away from us now?' He buzzed his Private Secretary and instructed him to tell Mr McDonald to come in.

'I thought I'd come in after your visitor leaves, sir,' McDonald said somewhat nervously when he came in again.

'No, come in, my Director. You know the Minister of Works? As a matter of fact it is the Minister that wants you, D.E.'

'Yes, sir?' the Englishman said inquiringly to the Minister of Works. He appeared to be making an effort to place the face.

'Please sit down, D.E., sit down.' Then turning to Moses he said, 'Look, Minister, if you want something from D.E. you had better move your chair to allow him to sit more comfortably.'

'I'll even get up and offer him my own chair,' Moses said, rising up and offering his chair to the expatriate official.

'Please, don't disturb yourself, Minister,' Derek McDonald said. 'I'm perfectly comfortable here, sir.'

'It is this letter, Director,' Hon. Anjorin handed the official envelope to McDonald. 'I don't understand the grammar you people write in the letter,' he continued as the official glanced through the sheets. 'But the Minister of Works does not like it at all.'

'I see,' McDonald said, looking up from the papers he held in his hand. He quickly drew out a white handkerchief from the pocket of his white shorts. Into this he exploded in a loud sneeze.

'But why do you write a letter like this to the Minister?' the Minister of Education asked, feigning rebuke.

'I beg your pardon, sir, but this letter is written to the

proprietors of Newtown Grammar School,' McDonald said, looking sideways at Moses, genuinely wondering what his objection could be.

'As if you don't know the Honourable Alade Moses, B.A. Dip.Ed., Minister of Works,' the Minister of Education said importantly.

'Minister, you flatter me,' Moses protested, lighting his second cigarette.

'Newtown Grammar School; the Hon. Alade Moses,' Mr Anjorin continued, smiling mischievously. 'The two are one and the same thing. So whatever you do to the Grammar School you do to the Minister. And whatever you do to the Minister you do to the Grammar School. You now see the position, my brother?' He too lit a cigarette.

'Yes, sir?' the Englishman said, still inquiringly. Either he had not understood or did not appreciate the argument.

'And what can you do for me, my Director?' Moses asked.

'I'm sure I don't see what I can do, sir. But is it true, sir, that you do not have a headmaster who possesses a university degree or the Board of Education Diploma? This is what this letter seems to imply – pardon me!' Mr McDonald cried as he twitched his whole body before exploding in another sneeze.

Moses nodded agreement with the official's observation.

'Apparently you had a headmaster who fulfilled these conditions – er – twenty-one months ago. Where's he gone to? Minister, find him. I myself will help you track him down and bring him back to your school. It is against the policy of the Ministry that school headmasters should migrate from school to school. No stability whatsoever. The thing must stop. In which school is the fellow now, Minister? We will bring him back to Newtown.'

The two politicians looked at each other ominously. Then Hon. Anjorin said: 'D.E., you don't seem to understand.

The Minister here *was* the Principal of Newtown Grammar School.'

'The hell he was – oh, I beg your pardon, sir,' McDonald said in confusion and embarrassment. He recollected then that Geoffrey Shepherd, the Principal of the Government-owned State College, had told him of this man who had left Newtown Grammar School for appointment as a Minister of State. So this was the chap!

'You now see, Minister,' the Hon. Anjorin said, yawning. 'The Director of Education did not remember that you were the Principal when he wrote this letter – who's it?' He screwed up his face at his Private Secretary who entered without knocking and started whispering something into his left ear. 'Who? Why will these people not leave me alone? What crime have I committed that they are for ever hunting for my blood? Minister, is this what your own constituency people do to you? They want me to build a pulpit of marble for my Church. They want me to fit every school leaver in my town in Government service. They want me to open the bazaar at the Harvest of every church in the town!'

'They are worse in my own Constituency,' Moses affirmed.

'No; impossible. None can be worse than my own Constituency. The God of Africa has given me the worst constituency on the continent. Look, you hear me,' he addressed his secretary. 'Tell him I'm not in – oh, he'd seen my car outside. Tell him I'm with the Prime Minister. We are holding a Cabinet meeting. Yes, tell, him that! Now, where was I? In this other matter oh ho! My Director will now withdraw this letter. He in fact was not the writer; you see —' he screwed up his face in an effort to identify the signature. 'You B.A. and M.A. people, when you sign your signatures, we Standard VI boys must run away.'

The two politicians laughed. This encouraged the Minister of Education to continue. 'But why can't you two friends agree, eh? You are B.A. (Hons.). The Minister of

Works, too, is B.A. (Hons.). When you academicians don't agree among yourselves, what should we laymen do, eh?'

'I'm rather worried, sir,' the unfortunate Englishman confessed. 'I'd like to do anything for the Minister, sir. But this is beyond me. I am not competent to authorize a contravention of the Education Code. The power to amend it is vested only in the Cabinet. A memorandum will have to go to the Cabinet from you, Minister. It is all a high policy matter. Should I tell the Permanent Secretary to see you, sir?'

'Permanent Secretary my foot,' the Minister of Education fumed, throwing the cigarette he was smoking at the framed map on the wall. 'When I say I want something in this Ministry, I want it, do you hear, Mr McDonald. This letter you wrote to Newtown Grammar School did not have my authority. It is hereby withdrawn. Now. Do you hear, Mr McDonald?'

'I hear, sir, but Minister —'

'I shall not stand any more insolence from any Civil Servant, white or black, you hear?' The Minister rose panting with fury.

'Very well, sir,' the Englishman said, retreating anxiously from the room.

'And Minister,' Hon Anjorin addressed his colleague, tearing up the letter, 'this matter is closed. And you,' he addressed his Private Secretary, who had rushed in the moment the Minister's voice had risen to anger pitch. 'Go and burn this. We shall know whether I am Minister of Education or whether that foolish, useless Englishman is.'

Nine

———————◇———————

IT was his expatriate friend Geoffrey Shepherd who first brought to his notice the problem of the State College project. Shepherd had told him that the Ministry of Education had been promised that the buildings would be completed for the beginning of the new school year starting in January. It was then May and the buildings had not been started. From inquiries he had made unofficially, the Treasury had finally approved the building vote and the delay now *appeared* to be in the Ministry of Works.

His Permanent Secretary told Moses that the contract for the project had been awarded and that work should be starting any time after that. The official then sent to him the green file marked 'SECRET' with 'TENDERS BOARD' stencilled in bolder characters. He was referred to p. 29 in that file. Turning to that page he read:

'H.M.W., you wanted information about the State College contract. As I told you, the D.P.W. has confirmed that the contract has already been awarded to the firm of Alberto Fernando. Kindly see p. 22 of this file for the minutes of the Tenders Board which awarded the contract. I am glad that the contract has been awarded as work can start immediately now on the construction. The Director of Education told me the other day of the very serious congestion at State College and the need for doing the new buildings quickly. Alberto Fernando are one of the leading firms of contractors in the country and are sure to do a fine job. I am pressing the Treasury for release of funds. I shall keep you informed. J.S. Stanfield. P.S.W.'

He turned to page 22 of the file for the details.

'Minutes of the meeting of the Tenders Board held in the Committee Room of the Treasury on Friday 23rd February, 1962. Present were' – here followed five names, three of them official and expatriate. Of these, he recognized one, that of Harrington the Director of Public Works. The other two names were of parliamentarians which rather surprised Moses, as he did not know that non-officials took part in such matters. The names of three other officials were recorded as being in attendance. 'Tenders for the construction of the new buildings of State College were considered. The tendering contractors and their tenders are as follows:

(a)	Gilbertson (West Africa) Ltd:	£220,050
(b)	Harris Construction Ltd:	£217,550
(c)	Hertz of Hamburg Ltd:	£195,000
(d)	Alberto Fernando Ltd:	£178,000
(e)	Niger Enterprises Ltd:	£112,000
(f)	A.B.C. Contractors:	?

'The Director of Public Works explained that there were two other tenders that did not satisfy the requirements for technical reasons. He placed them before the Board for a formal decision. He explained that the tender of A.B.C. Contractors was prepared in a most amateurish manner and showed evidence of a complete lack of knowledge of what a tender was.

'The Board considered at length the tender of Niger

Enterprises. The unofficial members expressed the desire to see the contract go to an indigenous contractor whose tender was considered reasonable, being in fact £66,000 lower than the next best tender. The Director of Public Works, however, explained that Niger Enterprises' tender was most unrealistic. The Ministry's estimate for the work was £215,000. It was obvious that no contractor could do the work for the figure quoted by Niger Enterprises and at the same time produce good work. If Government should award the contract to Niger Enterprises he was sure the contractors would discover that they had made a mistake in their tender and would then ask Government for more money or go bankrupt. Asked if the contractors (Niger Enterprises) had a good record with his Ministry the Director of Public Works said that they were fair on small jobs but that the State College project was completely beyond them.

'The Board eventually decided to award the contract to the next best contractor, namely Messrs Alberto Fernando Ltd. for the sum of £178,000. The Director of Public Works assured the Board of the very good standing of the contractors, which one of the unofficial members confirmed from personal knowledge of the work of the contractors.'

He read a few more pages in the file. From this he got more background information about the State College project. Letters showing the accommodation required by the Ministry of Education, estimates from the Ministry of Works, and instructions to the Ministry of Education from the Treasury that only £120,000 was available and that the Ministry of Works should be requested not to go beyond this amount. The letter from the Treasury directed the attention of all Accounting Officers to the relevant Treasury circular against over-expenditure.

Moses reflected on the time-consuming procedure of transacting government business. The Ministry of Works was only a minute's walk away from the Ministry of Education. He had heard that a letter written from the Ministry of Works might not be received for days at the registry of the Ministry of Education. Then it might take days, sometimes weeks, before the file in which it had been put materialised on the desk of the action officer. And it might be days, and sometimes weeks, before this officer burrowed deep enough to reach it in his 'pending' tray!

That night he communicated the good news to Geoffrey Shepherd. He invited the latter to come and have drinks with him five days after.

But this same State College contract was the cause of an emergency meeting of the Ministerial Committee in the office of Chief Franco-John in the Ministry of Justice three days after.

After the usual jokes about Ministers and their girl-friends, Franco-John told his colleagues that the Prime Minister had directed that they should consider the award of the State College contract in the light of Government's policy of encouraging African enterprise. This gave Moses the first hint that something had gone amiss.

'State College contract?' Town Planning repeated after the Attorney General enquiringly, his briar pipe drooping from the corner of his mouth.

'Yes,' the Attorney General said, fidgeting nervously with his second cigarette. 'The Ministry of Works has awarded the contract for State College to – er – Fernando Alberto Ltd.'

'Alberto Fernando Ltd., not Fernando Alberto Ltd.,' Moses corrected.

'Alberto Fernando, I'm sorry for the mistake, Minister,' Franco-John apologised.

'Alberto Fernando. Fernando Alberto. What is the difference?' Town Planning commented. He appeared to be joking, but the truth was that Kofi Kojo's educational background was poor and the horizon of his knowledge much limited.

'Fernando Alberto —'

'Alberto Fernando, Minister,' Moses quickly corrected Franco-John again before he went too far.

'Alberto Fernando is a foreign firm,' Franco-John announced, lighting his third cigarette.

'Alberto Fernando is a foreign firm,' Town Planning repeated after him, trying to see the implication of this.

After a few moments' silence the Minister of Home Affairs observed that he had heard of the firm before from the Roman Catholic Bishop who said that they were very good contractors and that they built the new science laboratory and chapel of the Mission's leading school in the Eastern Region and were about to start on the construction of the new mission hospital there as soon as the contract was signed.

The clock on the wall chimed the quarter to the hour. The air conditioner droned on noisily.

'You see, the P.M. is anxious that this Government support African enterprise. We must use our position to encourage our Afromacolese contractors,' the Attorney General gave a guiding lead to the discussion.

'Then why should we award this contract to Alberto Fernando, or Fernando Alberto. I suggest we award it to Abiola and Sons. They are good contractors,' Local Government suggested.

'Abiola and Sons,' Town Planning repeated, considering the implications, and chewing at the stem of his pipe. The moisture on his bald forehead shone.

'I know they are good contractors. But I think they are not as good as . . .' The name the Minister of Home Affairs mentioned was drowned by the combined noise of the air-conditioner and the ringing of the telephone.

After he had finished speaking on the phone, Franco-John explained to his colleagues that it wasn't a question of their looking for a contractor at that moment. They had gone beyond that stage because the Tenders Board had already advertised for tenders and received tenders for the work. Tenders had already closed and any contractor who did not send in a tender to the Tenders Board could not be considered for the contract. The Minister of Works could explain these things better.

Town Planning felt relieved at the prospect of explanation to come. Tenders. Tenders Board. Advertisement for Tenders. All these were incomprehensible to him.

For some eight minutes Moses explained to his colleagues this background, and all that he himself knew about tenders and tenders procedure. He emphasised that he himself had been worried that the contract had gone to an expatriate firm and had taken the opportunity to educate himself on the whole subject. He was very much interested in the case of Niger Enterprises and had pressed his Permanent Secretary for a reconsideration of the decision of the Tenders Board. But he had been told by his experts that this was impossible. The decision of the Board had already been communicated to Messrs Alberto Fernando and published in the official government gazette. To reverse the decision would involve the Government in litigation – Alberto Fernando would surely take Government to court for breach of contract. And they would most likely win their case. Besides it would be bad publicity for Government. This they could not afford, particularly at that time as they depended much on the support and co-operation of foreign governments.

He explained further that the composition of the Tenders Board was tied up with the need for its operations to be insulated from politics while at the same time the Legislature had a direct say in who got the contracts. There were three official members, all senior civil servants, with great experience and knowledgeable in contract practice and contract procedure. The unofficial members were chosen from a panel of unofficial members of the House of Assembly. No special order was followed in the selection of the two members for any particular meeting. And these two members were summoned by telegram forty-eight hours before the meeting. They did not know each other till they met at the meeting. They did not see the papers till they arrived at the meeting. They therefore did not know details of the contract they were being called to consider, nor which contractors were being considered. The contractors themselves did not know which two out of the sixty-six unofficial members of the House would be called to attend a particular meeting. All these precautions ensured that corruption was absolutely eliminated. Absolutely? Well – cut to the very minimum.

He sat back in his chair after this explanation. He had taken care not to mention his own personal prejudice against Geo Abyssinia. How could a man run a school and a contracting business together? He was satisfied that those competent to decide had decided against him. The Ministry of Works officials and the Tenders Board knew what they were talking about.

They listened to this explanation by Moses, with varying degrees of assent.

'Well, quite obviously what has been done has been done,' Home Affairs was the first to speak. 'We cannot change the decision of the Tenders Board, you see?'

'Yes, but we still don't seem to be taking into consideration the Prime Minister's directive on the Party's policy of the encouragement of African enterprise,' again the Attorney General emphasised the guideline for the meeting.

73

'Ah, that's the point, Minister,' Home Affairs faced Moses. 'How are you going to defend the award of this contract in the light of the Prime Minister's directive – and the Party's policy?' In matters of importance like this Roy Simpson was known to change his stand to suit the stand of whoever spoke last.

Someone wondered why Moses had taken the advice of his Permanent Secretary so seriously.

'Shouldn't I take him seriously?' Moses asked. 'He's there to advise me. Besides he in turn was advised by the Director of Public Works.'

'Both expatriates!' Education hissed.

'That's the point,' Franco-John said, crushing the end of a cigarette.

'Ah, these expatriates,' Home Affairs sighed.

'The Minister of Works appears to me to have allowed his expatriate officials to persuade him to support a decision which is in clear contradiction of our Party policy —'

'Look, you chaps think my Permanent Secretary just told me to do this and I did it,' Moses said, obviously annoyed. 'For your information I called in Theo George —'

'Theo George, Theo George, who's he?'

'Theo George is the most senior Afromacolese engineer in the Ministry. I sought his advice. He told me that the tender of Alberto Fernando was the best.'

'You see?' Home Affairs commented.

'Better than the tender of Niger Enterprises?'

'Yes.'

'Theo George told you that, Minister?' Franco-John asked.

'Indeed Theo George has some terrible things to say about Niger Enterprises and about Geo Abyssinia the Managing Director.'

Then the telephone rang. Franco-John stared at it for a moment before picking up the receiver. 'Yes, yes. From the

74

High Court? Yes, yes. What? You mean it? Lost, do you say? Are you sure? Yes, straight away. Moses and I will be coming to your office straight away.' After replacing the receiver Franco-John announced that the High Court had found against Moses in the libel action.

Ten

$\diamond$

THEO GEORGE, Acting Senior Engineer in the Ministry of Works, was with Alade Moses in his study when Geoffrey Shepherd's ancient Citroen drew up in the drive. George tried to rush through his explanations to the Minister before Shepherd came in. Both of them noticed that Shepherd was taking a long time coming in. So Moses shouted his name from the study.

'Sheep?' Moses called.

'Yes, Minister,' Shepherd answered from the car porch outside.

'Good heavens, what the hell are you doing out there?' Moses cried, coming out.

'I know you have someone with you. So I told the orderly not to bother you till you've finished with your visitor,' Shepherd explained, wiping his shoes on the door-mat before coming in.

'But what crime have I committed that all my friends are deserting me?' he said, shaking Shepherd's hand heartily. 'First Theo George. He wouldn't come to me till I had gone down on my knees to beg him. And now you, Sheep. Is it a crime to become a Minister of State?'

Shepherd and George exchanged greetings.

'As I was explaining to Theo George before you came in,

Sheep, if my official problems are complicated by my personal friends deserting me, I'll probably end up committing suicide. And that will be a neat solution to the whole problem from the point of view of Dauda – ha! ha! ha!'

Moses knew that his mention of Dauda would automatically make his companions think of the libel case which he had lost. The result was published in the papers the day after the judgement. It was just briefly mentioned in the foreign-owned local paper, but made the front page in the opposition paper. 'I see none of you has seen fit to congratulate me on the result of the libel case,' Moses said casually.

'Congratulate you?' Theo George repeated, enquiringly.

'Yes, congratulate me,' Moses confirmed.

'I hope it doesn't affect you seriously, Alade,' Shepherd asked. 'You know, damages and things.'

'That's the point. It was really a Party affair. It was Dauda versus the Freedom For All Party. Dauda against Freedom. If I had won, the Party would have reaped all the benefit. And now that I've lost the Party will pay the damages.'

'Really?' Theo George asked, surprised.

'Really. The Party paid the expenses. It will now pay the damages. Of course we are appealing against the judgement.'

'You are?'

'Of course we are. How can we allow one individual to stand against freedom and get away with it. Dauda versus freedom. Can't you see? Ha! ha! ha!'

They all laughed.

The steward came to ask what drinks each person wanted. Shepherd asked for bitter lemon, George for Star beer.

'Star, beer at its best,' Moses repeated the famous beer advert.

'And what are you taking yourself, Alade?' Shepherd asked.

'The usual,' Moses said.

'Cider?'

'Yes, cider. The only drink worth taking in this cursed place.'

'I know you were very fond of cider in London, Alade. But I hear the stuff is frightfully expensive here. I wonder why most drinks are so expensive,' Shepherd said.

'Do you really wonder? I tell you why. Our Government is to blame. Stealing the people's money. That's just what it is,' Moses declared, obviously enjoying the joke he was making at the expense of the Government of which he was a member.

They all laughed. Then Shepherd excused himself to go to the lavatory George went to the telephone to try to reach his own house.

Left alone, Moses pondered from where he sat the things that bound him and the Englishman together. They had met during the Diploma in Education year at the School of African and Oriental Studies in London. That was two and a half years before. Geoffrey Shepherd had been an Education Officer in Her Majesty's Colonial Service for nine years before then. The first three of these he had spent in Nyasa-land and all the remaining six in Afromacoland. It was after this that he had been sent on an in-service training scholarship to London, to try out in company of some two dozen senior education officers from the scattered territories of the British Commonwealth the new ideas in education for overseas territories which an erudite professor in Oxford had been serializing in learned journals for eighteen months. Alade Moses was one of the five African students in the class and both he and Sheep (as Shepherd was popularly called at College) clicked at their first meeting in London. Back in Afromacoland, Geoffrey Shepherd was promoted to Principal of the Government Secondary School, State College, in Victoria at the same time that Alade Moses was appointed Principal of the Newtown Grammar School.

He had first met Theo George in London, at meetings of the Afromacolese Students Union of Great Britain. There Theo George was known for the number of papers he read at conferences on subjects like the reorganization of the civil service, industrialization in a developing country, and corruption. He had taken six years doing his first degree in engineering instead of the normal three. After three years' service in Victoria he had been sent back for a year's postgraduate course with the Crown Agents in their Civil Engineering Design Division under the country's scheme for accelerated training for Afromacolese to assume senior posts. It was when he was doing the course with the Crown Agents that Moses had met George. Moses was himself Treasurer of the Students Union. When Moses was Principal of Newtown Grammar School he and George had kept fairly well in touch with each other. They had both discovered that the exacting work they each did left them little time to devote to the affairs of the Students Union, which they had faithfully promised to do before they left Britain. Moses was the first to discover that a number of the ideas they had as students in Britain were just impracticable in Afromacoland. Now that Moses was a Minister of State and in charge of the Ministry in which George was a senior officer, he decided that he would consult him unofficially on some of the things that the Permanent Secretary and the Director of Public Works – both of them expatriates – placed before him.

When the three of them were assembled once more, Moses declared: 'You see sitting with you here the most miserable individual in all God's creation.'

'How's that, Minister?' George asked.

'How? Now I see Sheep, I recall our days together at the S.O.A.S. in London. The things we planned together. The things we were to do together back home here in Afromacoland. But see me now —'

Both his visitors understood. They said nothing. Shepherd fiddled with the ash tray, while Moses appeared lost in his own thoughts.

'I wanted to be Minister of Education. But the Prime Minister wanted me to be Minister of Works. And my constituency – they too wanted me to be Minister of Works —'

'But Works is a most important Ministry, Alade,' Shepherd said, quite seriously.

'This is what I've been trying to impress upon the Minister all these years,' George said. 'It would be disastrous to have any of those others as Minister of Works. Why, that chap Kojo wouldn't understand a thing in the Ministry.'

'And I know that you will put me through, Theo. Showing me the ropes, and teaching me bridge construction and water supply. And mathematics – ha, ha, ha. Too late, I'm afraid, too late to force mathematics through my thick skull.'

'One wonders if the new Government will continue with the proposals for universal primary education,' Shepherd observed. 'Now they have an expert on education I'm sure they'll think twice,' he grinned at Moses.

'I quite understand,' Moses said. 'They say in Afromacolese language that the reason why you speak in the presence of the child of a deaf man is to make him hear what you say.'

'Quite true, quite true,' George observed.

'I'm going to be frank, Alade, but you know as I do that while universal primary education is a most worthy objective, a goal we must arrive at eventually, it's sheer lunacy to think that we are going to wipe out illiteracy in Afromacoland in one decade.'

'Oh yes,' Alade commented thoughtfully.

'And this has nothing to do with the set ideas of McDonald, nothing to do —'

'Ah, McDonald,' Moses said reflectively. 'I fear your Minister was quite rough with him the day we discussed my successor at Newtown Grammar School. I was quite embarrassed.'

'Old Mac has forgotten all about it. Nothing bothers him. So long he gets his regular double shot of whisky, he's quite happy.'

'Really?' Moses asked, surprised.

'Really. And I shouldn't bother about him over much.'

'Oh dear, I think Anjorin was quite unreasonable with him,' Moses said into his glass of cider. 'Now back to the question of universal primary education, we politicians are confusing two different things. The adult education campaign will take care of illiteracy. That too will take a long time but not too long. It is the question of universal primary education that is a serious matter. A most formidable problem.'

'Formidable is an understatement, Alade,' Shepherd puffed at his pipe sagely. 'Impossible in our own life-time. Absolutely impossible. Think of the sheer immensity of the problem. No record of births and deaths – no statistics of any kind. Therefore no knowledge of the number of children we must provide for in the primary schools. If however the 1963 census figures and the 1967 projection from them are anything to go by then we may reckon on something like one and a half million children of primary school age in this country. And you know what that means.'

'One and a half million children,' Moses commented.

'One and a half million children,' Shepherd repeated. 'The school accommodation for a start. At thirty-five kids to a class and six classes per school you have two hundred and ten per school. Say two hundred, allowing for five per cent wastage. That gives how many schools?'

'Seven hundred – seven thousand and five hundred,'

George did the mental arithmetic. Moses listened, most absorbed.

'Seven thousand, five hundred schools. The 1952 Census showed eight hundred and forty-seven elementary schools already existing in the country. Eleven per cent of requirement. Eighty-seven per cent of these are owned and run by the missions. That's just by the way. What's important is that we shall require over six thousand new schools.'

'Six thousand new schools,' Moses muttered, nodding.

'The Director of Public Works tells us that each school can be expected to cost £3,000. On your building programme alone you require . . .' Shepherd looked at George for the answer.

'Eighteen million pounds!' George did the sum.

'Eighteen million pounds!' Moses repeated, obviously impressed.

'Yes, eighteen million pounds,' Shepherd strung out the words for greater effect.

'I suppose this could be done in a five or six year development programme,' George observed.

'Which means an expenditure of three million pounds a year on primary school buildings alone. Yet all our vote for capital expenditure on all forms of education in the 1963/64 year is one hundred and twenty-seven thousand pounds. One hundred and twenty-seven thousand, not one million two hundred and seventy thousand pounds!' He adjusted himself in the chair apparently preparing for following up the implication of the statistics. But the telephone rang. He took the advantage of Moses' absence at the telephone to charge his pipe with tobacco from a pouch he produced from the seat pocket of his outsize khaki shorts. His white linen shirt was already wet with perspiration, the form of the vest under being clearly visible in front. George noticed that his forearms and the portions of his thighs and knees between the shorts and his stockings were tanned, the sure trade mark of Englishmen who had stayed in West Africa for many years.

'But money is just one of the problems,' he continued after Moses had returned from the telephone. He paused for some time, looking at George as a teacher would look at a pupil from whom he expected a bright idea.

'The teachers?' George said, wondering if this was what the educationist had in mind. Moses said nothing, but appeared lost in his own thoughts.

'Yes, the teachers,' Shepherd continued. 'At eight per school, and for – er —'

'Seven thousand five hundred schools.'

'Seven thousand five hundred schools. You need – er – sixty thousand of them. They don't grow on trees. You have to find them. You have to train them. Train fifty per cent of them. Or even twenty-five per cent,' he said slowly. The other two men were apparently following his argument.

'Teacher training, a most interesting subject – the teaching of those that will teach in the schools. The building of teacher training colleges and the recruitment of the teachers that will teach the teachers that will teach in the elementary schools. We will build the foundations and the walls of concrete and blocks. They need cement. We shall build the roofs with iron sheets and fasten them to the roof timber with nails. There is not a single factory in this country producing cement or iron sheets or nails.'

George saw a slight frown darken the brow of Moses. He was worried that he was going to take Shepherd to task on this point of non-industrialization of the country on which African nationalists felt so strongly. It would be most embarrassing to have Shepherd and a Minister of State involved in a serious argument in his own house. But to his relief it was Moses himself who introduced yet another of the serious obstacles in the way of universal primary education. 'We must not overlook the sociological factors either,' he said, crushing the remains of his cigarette in the ash-tray. 'There's going to be the question of unemployment when the boys and girls begin to come off the production line after the six years primary education course for all.'

'Quite a serious thing, planning for the hundred thousand or so kids that must flood the employment market every year,' George commented.

'Unemployment. The disease of the industrialized, so-called developed countries. Till now your country has been shielded from this by-product of our civilization, Minister,' Shepherd snatched at the subject. 'Unemployment, with its ally the inevitable drift from the villages to the towns. Crime and juvenile delinquency. Total disorganization of happy family life. Detribalization. My God – if only your people knew the dangerous toy with which they are playing. And I am not underrating the intelligence of the truly educated African – and I know quite a few like you, Alade – when I say that like children your people need protection against the dangers of this toy known as universal primary education. I am sure, Alade, you will steer your colleagues clear of these dangers.'

That night he dreamt about universal primary education, adult education, and teacher training. He was Minister of Education and he organized them all. He dreamt about Newtown Grammar School. He was still Principal, even though he was Minister of Education; and he was Minister of Works as well. In fact in his dream he ran the whole government – making political speeches all over the place, and giving instructions to all and sundry, expatriate and indigenous. Then there was an election petition case against him. Dauda was the petitioner. 'I accuse this man standing there of gross election frauds and mass cheating of the electorate of this land,' Abdul Dauda, his accuser, had said in his thunderous voice before the High Court Judge in the dream. 'And I demand that he be hanged by the neck till he be dead.'

'Alade Moses of Newtown, you have been accused of gross election frauds and mass cheating of the electorate of this land. What is your plea, guilty or not guilty?' he heard the judge say in a very grave voice.

'Guilty, my Lord,' he heard himself say. Then Gloria woke him, telling him that he'd been saying incoherent things in his troubled sleep.

Eleven

ALADE MOSES allowed the telephone to ring on. Six-thirty in the morning. No doubt another constituency man, wanting to be made a contractor in the Ministry of Works. Or another party man from another constituency, wanting an appointment. He would be armed with a note of introduction from a Minister colleague who would vouch for his ability to construct the most complex work of civil engineering. Or maybe an influential member of the powerful Newtown Improvement Union. Wanting an introduction to the expatriate Managing Director of the United Africa Enterprises for greater credit facilities. All the hours of the day, all the days of the week – Sundays not excepted – in his office, at home, he interviewed them. He listened to their problems, and to their complaints. And at night he dreamt of them. He had now had nearly eleven months of this terrible life. Now he was getting fed up. Let the caller go to hell this time. He lay on his back, watching a gecko stalking an unsuspecting moth on the white ceiling of his bedroom.

Presently his steward knocked at the door.

'Who is it?'

'Me, Master.'

'Yes?'

'It's Madam, Master.'

'Madam?'

Gloria had been with him till mid-night. He had driven her to the hospital himself. So she couldn't have come to any harm on the way, he was sure. But why was she ringing so early?

'Hello Glor,' he yawned into the receiver.

'I see you are still feeling sleepy. I'm sorry to wake you up.'

'That's all right, Glor. I've been awake for some time, as a matter of fact.'

'Why then didn't you want to speak to me?'

'I thought it was one of my usual clients ringing. Why are you calling so early, anyway? Trying to compensate for your naughtiness?'

'Have you seen the papers?'

'Which papers?'

'The *Sentinel*.'

'No. Why?'

'They say there's trouble in the Party and that there is a big quarrel between you and Chief Franco-John. I haven't seen it myself, but Sister Isaac told me about it. Is it really so serious? Why are you keeping it from me? You won't even answer me now?'

He did not say anything. He had for the last few days been moody, saying little about his difficulties. She had tried to make him talk. She had tried to cheer him up. His response to her allurements had been more mechanical than usual. She was worried. She burst into tears on the telephone.

A few minutes later, Moses read the screaming headline in the *Sentinel*: 'Serious Crack in Government Party Front: Franco-John versus Alade Moses.'

He read on: 'All is not well in the Government Party. The gulf that has opened between the Attorney General and the Minister of Works over the State College Building Contract widened further in the last forty-eight hours and matters have now reached a point where one or the other of the two Ministers must go.

'It is believed that Mr Alade Moses has become more and more critical of Government's policies and activities and that he has by his actions embarrassed his ministerial colleagues several times. Well-informed sources say that the young, honest ex-schoolmaster has been unable to reconcile both the policies of the Cabinet and the activities of his colleagues with the promises the Party made to the electorate. It is a well known fact that he is a man of ability and integrity. But this is precisely why he is in difficulty in a Party which has no place for men of ability and honour and which places a premium on dishonesty and squandermania.

'It is understood that Party Elders have been summoned to an emergency meeting with the Parliamentary Committee of the Party tonight. It is believed that pressure will be brought on Alade Moses to toe the party line. But those of us who know the once hard-hitting Treasurer of the Afromacolese Students Union of Great Britain know that he will rather resign than compromise himself where issues of honour are involved as in this case.

'We of this paper know the difficulties our Prime Minister faces. An honest man himself, he has left too much in the hands of his Attorney General and Minister of Agriculture, who in fact runs the Government. Of him we shall say nothing. The Electorate see and understand everything. It will be asking too much of the Prime Minister to read the writing on the wall: his reading glasses have long been taken away by the very man that will very soon lead him and the nation to disaster unless something is done now.

'We wait and see how the Party resolves the crisis within its fold.'

The Elders and the Parliamentary Committee of the Party looked into the matter. The meeting was held in the large sitting room of the official residence of the Prime Minister. He explained the purpose of the meeting. He had been worried for some time about the way his Ministers had been quarrelling among themselves. He of course knew that people who were thrown together in any form of association would have different approaches to the same problem. No two people could see the same matter exactly the same way. What was required was understanding and a willingness to listen to the other man's point of view and an explanation of your own point. This was what he had tried to impress upon his colleagues, the need to appreciate each other's point of view and to strike a balance. He was worried that he had spent much time in settling quarrels between his Ministers. The matter was assuming serious proportions and was getting out of hand. 'I am now very much worried about the thing. No peace within the Party. No peace in the Cabinet. And the Opposition leaves no stone unturned to inflame public opinion against us. This is the position. So I decided to call this meeting. I confess I am no longer master of the situation. You Elders put us in charge of this Government. It is said that when there are old and experienced women in the market they cannot allow a situation where a young and inexperienced mother carries her baby on her back with its head not properly supported. It is your own saying, Elders, I do not presume to arrogate to myself the wisdom of you Elders.'

No one spoke for some time after the Prime Minister had finished speaking. No one appeared to be in a hurry to speak. They all looked at one another as if they knew that great responsibility attached to whatever was said after Chief the Honourable Dr Bandele Ogun. Franco-John smoked pensively where he sat. Alade Moses stared at the ceiling with his arms folded across his chest.

'Well Elders, this is the position,' the Prime Minister primed his guests. 'This is what we've been facing. If I had known that this was the type of support I was going to get from my colleagues, I confess I wouldn't have abandoned the medical profession to head the Government. Frankly speaking I'm disappointed. Very much disappointed. So I want you Elders, and you Ministers, to settle this matter today. Are we to go forward as a well disciplined body for the achievement of our purpose? Or are we to continue in this disgraceful manner? Perhaps you'll want Chief Franco-John to speak first.'

After some silence one of the Elders said: 'We must thank the P.M. for calling this meeting. We must. I tell you why we must,' he looked around their faces and nodded, apparently in satisfaction with himself at what he was saying. 'It is true we are all Party men. We started this Party together. But in spite of that supposing the P.M. refuses to call us here – supposing he says he's now the P.M. and will have nothing to do with us commoners, what can we do?'

One or two heads nodded approval of the observation and agreement about the reasonableness of the Prime Minister in associating these outsiders with an important affair of the Government.

'But Elders you are our fathers,' the Minister of Local Government said. 'We are glad that P.M. decided to call you to our rescue. Fathers, why if even we are made Ministers a hundred times over is it not you who put us there? Is it not you, I ask?'

While one elder nodded in appreciation, another observed that it was the votes of the people that put the Ministers in their exalted position.

'Votes of the people?' Local Government commented dryly. 'Why, who are the people? Who are behind the people? I want to ask a question. If Chief Odole should declare today that he's withdrawing his support from Alade Moses, will all Newtown not follow his lead against Moses? Don't let us deceive ourselves. Fathers, you are our support. And we must recognize the fact. In fact we do recognize it. And that's why we have brought our trouble to you.'

Silence again. Franco-John smoked on. Alade Moses now stared at the horizon via one of the windows in the sitting room. He noticed that some wrought-iron burglar-proofing had been erected over the window. Quick work by Harrington's men. It was only three days before that he told the Permanent Secretary that the Senior Intelligence Officer had recommended that security arrangements in the Prime Minister's Lodge be stepped up. There was some gossip that the Opposition were planning to assassinate him. Fantastic, but nothing was to be left to chance.

'Well, Minister? What's the cause of the trouble between you and Minister Alade Moses?' one of the Elders addressed Franco-John.

'Trouble between me and Alade Moses? None whatsoever.' Franco-John crushed the remains of a cigarette in the ash-tray.

At this point, the Prime Minister's Private Secretary came in, with a file under his arm. He tip-toed to the Prime Minister and knelt beside his chair to whisper something to his ears. Whatever the importance or otherwise of what the civil servant was telling him the impassive face of the politician did not indicate. After some time, he stretched out his left hand for the file his Secretary brought. After reading through a page in it he nodded to his Secretary who took the file and tip-toed out of the room.

'P.M., Minister Franco-John won't say anything. Shall we beg him? Minister, we beg you to tell us anything that is on your mind. We want to settle this matter now. Today,' the same Elder pleaded.

'But fathers, I want to make a suggestion,' Local Government said. 'I beg you all to forgive my impertinence. I am a small boy among you. Six of us here are really too young to be at a sitting like this. Forget that we are Ministers. We are Ministers all right; but when we meet like this, we know who is who. Both Chief Franco-John and Chief Alade Moses . . .'

'Mister, please, Mister,' Alade Moses corrected.

'Well, Mister. But I choose to call you Chief. I don't see what the Newtown people are still doing that they have not yet made you a chief?' he observed humorously in the direction of Chief Odole. 'Still, as I was saying, both men are Senior Ministers. They are both university graduates. When on the day of judgement God is judging the case of the rich he will not allow the poor in the courthouse. My suggestion to you fathers is to take P.M., Chief Franco-John, and Chief Alade Moses to the P.M.'s bedroom and settle the matter up there.'

'Good talk, good talk,' the Minister of Town Planning commented.

'But leave the rest of us here with P.M.'s fridge and steward. We shall make ourselves comfortable.'

The telephone rang. Again the Principal Private Secretary tip-toed in and removed the receiver from the phone and placed it on the writing desk near by. He then tip-toed out of the room.

'Well, Chief Odole. This is word,' said the first Elder who had complimented the Prime Minister on associating himself and his colleagues with the matter in hand. He tapped his walking stick on the terrazzo floor.

'But P.M.,' Franco-John said, indicating with the cigarette in his hand the telephone receiver on the desk.

'Oh,' the Prime Minister sighed, removing the receiver and replacing it on the telephone. 'The efficiency of our Civil Servants,' he muttered.

'Sabotage, that's what it is,' one of the Ministers said. 'They are all in the pay of the Opposition. All of them.'

'A very good suggestion that we should go up to my bedroom, Elders. Please follow me upstairs,' and the Prime Minister rose to lead the way to his rooms.

But the Elder who had earlier observed that the Ministers owed their positions to the votes of the people said that he

92

wished to make one or two observations to the full house before they retired to tackle the particular problem of the trouble between Chief Franco-John and Alade Moses. He said that he was surprised that the young men remembered them, the Elders of the Party, after they had got into a scrape. He was surprised that they did not consider themselves all wise, almighty, so capable of settling all their problems. Why, when their Party won the election they had all held high hopes for the young men into whose hands the government of the people was being placed. 'We all went to the church for thanksgiving. We all prayed for the great Jehovah to lead you young men in your arduous tasks. We hoped that you would discharge your duties in the fear of the Lord and in respect for us the Elders. But what have we seen of you since you became important people? What have we seen of you?'

'Father. It is enough. Let us try . . .' Town Planning pleaded.

'Enough? D'you say enough? I shall say the words of my mouth. And if you don't like it you can stop calling me to a meeting like this tomorrow. When you began to earn big salaries and ride big cars did you not forget us your Elders? When you share the money which you make in the Government, do you remember us the Elders? I am rather surprised that this young man has such wisdom to suggest what he has suggested,' and here he indicated the Minister of Local Government. 'We Elders are not fools. We have worked and will continue to work for the Party. But we cannot continue to do this for nothing, while you young men carry away all the fruits of government.'

Eventually the three Elders, Franco-John and Alade Moses followed the Prime Minister upstairs.

Twelve

---◇---

'WELCOME, Your Excellency, welcome a thousand times,' the Honourable Franco-John said in a most charming manner as he took a few steps forward to meet the man climbing out of the back seat of the black Oldsmobile. A police constable saluted and then joined the chauffeur in white uniform with shining buttons, in holding the door open for the V.I.P. to come out.

'I apologise a thousand, thousand times, Hon. Minister,' the new arrival said in a strong Oriental accent as he shook the hand the Minister offered. He gave it a slight pressure and hugged the Minister with his free arm, all suggestive of comradeship and relationship extending beyond official association. He was a man with a small body and thin neck which carried a disproportionately big head. His face was freckled and highlighted by a military moustache. He wore an expensive blue suit out of the breast pocket of the coat of which showed the tip of a white silk handkerchief. 'I was held up by a telephone call from my Prime Minister.'

'Oh yes,' Franco-John said as he adjusted his steps to suit the shorter legs of his companion.

'Yes, Minister. From New York.'

'From New York?' Franco-John shot a side glance at him, inquiringly. 'Must be wonderful.'

'Yes, from New York, Minister. You know my Prime Minister is addressing the United Nations Assembly on Thursday this week. Just now he's very busy putting the finishing touches to his speech. He writes his own speeches by himself. Most particular about his choice of words. And the grammar.'

'Must be an interesting personality, your Prime Minister.'

'Interesting? Dedicated – a statesman of a high order, Minister. The personification of the soul, the – the – the embodiment of the struggle and aspirations of our new nation. You must meet our Prime Minister some day. I will arrange for your Prime Minister and you and another Minister to visit my country.'

'Your Excellency . . .'

'No, no, no, Minister. Just a small, infinitesimally small measure of the affection my Government has for you, the bond of friendship between our two nations, the – the – the . . .'

Now at the landing on the first floor the Minister preceded his guest through a double door which was held open by a constable and a steward in white.

'Ladies and Gentlemen, His Excellency the Jordarmenian Ambassador, Dr Mose Selisha,' Franco-John announced in formal tones.

The diplomat first stood at attention, then his face lit up with a big smile. He bowed stiffly, first to the left, then to the centre, and finally to the right.

The Minister of Town Planning was the third V.I.P. to be introduced to the diplomat. 'I quite understand your difficulties, my dear Minister,' the Jordarmenian Ambassador cried in a voice that drowned the chattering of the many guests in the big hall. A good number of the women looked up in curiosity. Two men exchanged furtive glances in a way only Britishers know how. 'I was once Minister of Town Planning in my own country. You don't have to preach to me about the problems of town planning and housing. They are the same the world over.'

'I am glad to hear that, sir. Very glad to hear you say so.' Town Planning failed to notice the frown on Franco-John's face – the senior Minister disapproved of the way his colleague addressed the ambassador as 'sir' as if he was admitting the superiority of either the country or the person of the ambassador. 'I hope you will give me some books to read on town planning in your country. I want to read all the books I can get on the subject of my portfolio.'

'Books! Of course I shall give you all the books you want. More than you can read really. I think you will find that we have in my country a number of standard works on the subject. Written by scholars of international fame – Ah, let's see now,' he said, examining critically a cigar he took from a box offered him by a steward.

'Thank you, thank you. May I send my Private Secretary to your office tomorrow to collect the books?'

'Collect the books – no, no, no! I'll present the books to you myself. And I'll present another set to your National Library. I'll have them suitably autographed by my Prime Minister himself. "Donated by the Government and people of Jordarmenia, in love and friendship, to the people of Afromacoland".'

Franco-John piloted his guest tactfully away from Town Planning. He said: 'Mr John Harrington, our Director of Public Works.'

'Mr Harrington, most delighted to meet you,' the ambassador said, looking penetratingly into the eyes of the British civil servant. The victim muttered something inaudible in a manner typical of his countrymen in such situations.

'Yours must be a most responsible job, Mr Harrington. Nothing is more important than public works in a developing country. I should know what I am talking about – I was Under Secretary in our Department of Public Works in our first coalition government.'

'Indeed,' Harrington muttered.

'And you must arrange to send a number of your engineers to see the achievements of my Government in the field of water supply and irrigation. This is one field in which all the world acclaims the superiority of my country.'

'Quite an achievement, Your Excellency,' Harrington muttered.

'The Honourable Minister of Works is not here yet,' Franco-John observed. 'Tell us, Mr Harrington, what have you done with your Minister?' he asked jokingly, selecting another cigarette from a box a steward held before him.

'My Minister was working late in the office this afternoon, Minister. He and the Permanent Secretary were busy over some papers for the Prime Minister, I think.'

'Ah, we shall soon know,' Franco-John said to himself as Gloria entered the hall. 'His girl-friend,' he whispered to the ambassador as he led him away from Harrington, much to the relief of the latter.

'You mean the girl that is just coming in, Minister?'

'The one in front, in native dress. She's a nursing sister in the General Hospital.'

'Useful to know, most useful information.'

They stayed to chat with one or two other guests before they reached the group to which Gloria had attached herself – a man in flowing white robes and three girls.

'I am cross with you for coming late to my party, Miss Oke. I'm sure it is deliberate. Done to spite a poor Minister of State,' Franco-John said, pretending to be truly cross with Gloria.

They all laughed as Gloria explained. It was due to an emergency case in the hospital. 'The Manager of Andrew Williams and Co. A very ghastly accident. Doctor had to perform an emergency operation.'

'And of course you had to be there, I know. Your Excellency, this is Miss Gloria Oke, Senior Nursing Sister at the General Hospital. His Excellency the Jordarmenian Ambassador in Afromacoland.'

'Most charmed, most honoured, most delighted to meet you, my charming lady! In the course of my travels through many countries in the world I have met many women. But I'm still to meet a woman more beautiful than the Afromacolese woman in her national attire.'

Gloria giggled at the compliment.

'I have also wondered why our women will not dress always in their native dress,' said the man in white robes, adjusting the sleeves of his agbada. 'Look at Miss Oke now. Does she not look beautiful in this native dress? You just look at her.'

'Excellent, Gorgeous. Perfect. You cannot conceive of anything more beautiful, more fitting, more – more – more stylish.' The diplomat stroked his whiskers for effect. One of the other two girls had slipped away in embarrassment. Apart from being less attractive than Gloria, she wore a blue frock. The other girl was dressed in a spotted 'up-and-down', a hybrid between the Ghanaian woman's national costume and the English woman's blouse and skirt.

The ambassador took two steps back noisily and subjected Gloria to a more formal, critical examination, the way you step back to admire more effectively a work of art hanging on the wall. Gloria was truly attractive and attractively dressed, the obviously exaggerated observations of Dr Mose Selisha notwithstanding. She wore a cream woollen Afromacolese blouse over a blue velvet lapper, the contours of her breasts showing invitingly through the blouse. She wore a striped silk head-tie in the famous 'onilegogoro' style. Her white handbag went very well with her white, stylish sandals. She did not have on excessive jewellery but her gold necklace and her earrings were obviously from the famous Hooper works.

'Perfect. Exquisite. Wonderful,' the diplomat pronounced. 'But what are you having, my fair lady? Steward, this way, this way. What can he get for you?'

'Sherry,' she said simply. At this point the remaining girl in the original group had spotted the Minister of Education who entered at that moment, and made for him.

'Sherry for the lady, steward. The very best for the best lady in all Victoria. Pity the stuff they serve in these places. Poison. That's what I call it. Poison.'

'The British don't know good drinks,' said the man in white robes. 'And they won't let us buy from France. Have you ever seen such dogs in the manger before?'

'A perfect description. Most apt, Mr – er –'

'Geo Abyssinia, Your Excellency,' Franco-John now introduced him. 'Chief Abyssinia is the Managing Director of the firm of Niger Enterprises Ltd., the leading firm of indigenous contractors in Victoria.'

'Most delighted to meet you, Your Excellency,' Abyssinia shook the ambassador's hand with much fuss.

'Contracting. Contracting. Which really is your speciality, Chief? Roads and bridges? Buildings? Water supply?' the Ambassador reeled off these subdivisions of civil engineering with ease.

'All. I'm interested in all. My firm is established in all parts of the Federation. And Minister, I really ought to come home to tell you the news. We won the tender for the construction of the Lafia High School in the North. I got the telegram today.'

'Excellent,' Franco-John exclaimed.

'Congratulations, Chief, congratulations,' the diplomat said, patting him on the shoulder.

'Congratulations, sir,' Gloria said in a soft voice.

'Thank you, my dear. I think I should congratulate you,

Minister, and you, cousin. And I congratulate the African. For I consider this not just an achievement for me as an individual contractor. It is an achievement for African enterprise. You know something, Minister?'

'Yes?'

'I won this contract, beating fourteen other bidders in the contest. Your European friends failed woefully this time.'

'They too competed?'

'Ask your colleagues in the Cabinet in the North. The Ministers up there are now seeing what we've been telling them all these years. The days of the white capitalist are numbered, Minister. Even the North are now seeing the light. But Minister, what are we doing here in this part of the country, we who used to lead the rest of the country in all things progressive? Minister, I fear to talk. Perhaps this is not the place for discussing this matter.'

'Ah, Chief, I'd like to have a word with you really. But we mustn't talk shop here. We must not bore Miss Oke,' Franco-John said.

'Oh, I'm all right,' she said, sipping her sherry.

'When a lady speaks like that you should understand her to mean the very opposite of what she says,' the ambassador observed. 'Why won't you two go and discuss business while this charming lady and I discuss the latest fashion in ladies dresses.'

'And the latest scandal in town,' the Minister said as he took the cue and led the contractor away.

'There must be a lot to do in your hospital. There's nothing as important as the organization of health services in any country. Particularly so in a new nation such as yours. And the emphasis must be on the training of nurses. Where were you trained, if I may ask?'

'In Britain. Queen Mary Hospital, in London.'

'London, London,' the diplomat said, waving away a

waiter that seemed to be bothering him with a tray of sausages. 'British nurse-training schemes are half a century out of date. Imagine the hospitals themselves. Old Victorian buildings reflecting the national character in their very dismal, depressing appearance. Stuck in squares with little or no ventilation. Modern Florence Nightingales cannot be produced or operate in such an atmosphere. But I'm sorry, Miss Okay, what will you have next?'

'Oh, I'm still all right.'

'You don't seem to be making much impression on that glass in your hand. I don't blame you. Any sherry that originates from Britain is poison. Wines from my country are famous the world over. I think I shall send you a carton of the real stuff tomorrow. My secretary will bring it to the hospital.'

'Oh no, sir!'

'Why?'

'At the hospital! Why, the whole town will be talking about it for the next six months. I beg you, don't send anything to me in the hospital, sir.'

'Of course I should know. You just leave it to me. Do let me order something else for you. Waiter, a shot of cointreau for the lady. Yes, cointreau. And bring it quick.'

It appeared as if all in the party had a common under-standing that the Jordarmenian Ambassador was not to be disturbed while he was with Gloria Oke. The chattering and babbling of voices continued. There was much giggling. The smell of tobacco hung heavily in the air of the room which the architects had sentenced to life-long staleness in the name of air-conditioning.

'A year or two in the Jordarmenian Teaching Hospital will do you a lot of good. The Nurses Training School has trained nurses for a good many of the developing nations of Africa and Asia. Quite a number of girls come from Central Europe and from Latin America.'

'The Hospital must be quite famous,' Gloria observed, excited.

'Famous? World wide recognition! I'll let you have an article done by a W.H.O. expert where he says the Jordarmenian Teaching Hospital is in a class by itself. Of course you will not have to do the ordinary course. What you will want with your experience is a concentrated post-graduate course. You will do a thesis in a special subject like the organisation of nursing services in a developing nation. We must have ladies like you to form the nucleus of my Government's projected aid to your country in this vital field.'

'Thank you,' she said, her excitement mounting.

'A scholarship to the Jordarmenian Teaching Hospital. What's the name again, my good lady?'

'Gloria Oke.'

'Gloria Okay – how beautiful. Beautiful in name, beautiful in appearance. One or two years in Jordarmenia. Scholarship arranged.'

'Thank you, sir,' Gloria said. She felt on top of the world.

'Thank me, for what? Why, this is no more than a mere token of the bond of friendship between your country and mine. A little measure of the appreciation of my Government for the wonderful hospitality of your people to Jordarmenian nationals in this country.'

Thirteen

MOSES heard all about the party from Gloria the following night. She told him of the promise of a scholarship to Jordarmenia and begged Moses to pursue the matter further with the Ambassador. She gave a detailed list of the girls that came to the party, what each of them wore and with which Minister or V.I.P. each of them came or went away. She ended up by coming back to the Ambassador and saying how wonderful she thought he was.

'You nearly make me jealous of him, Gloria,' Moses teased her. 'Are you telling me indirectly that you want to desert me for the Jordarmenian Ambassador?'

'Jealous man,' she said giggling. 'I thought you were incapable of being jealous.'

'Am I?'

'You said so yourself. Don't you remember?' She looked at him from where she still sat on the settee after the long warm embrace, before he got up to leave her ground floor flat in the hospital. It had been an all-too-short visit, but he had explained to her that he had an important appointment with the Prime Minister.

'You don't remember you told me that there is nothing I can do that will make you jealous?' She cocked her head coquettishly.

'Supposing I tell you I don't, what next?' He was fidgeting with his wrist watch, evidence that he was anxious to get away to the appointment with the Prime Minister. He noticed that she neither answered his question nor made any attempt to get up from the settee. He knew she was cross with him.

'Look, Glor, I really must go now. I mustn't keep the P.M. waiting,' he said anxiously.

'Who's stopping you, Mr Minister?'

'You are not seeing me to the car then?'

She neither replied nor made any attempt to get up from the settee. He sighed, took a few steps back to her, and settled down to another bout of warm embraces on the settee.

Later on their way to the car she asked: 'Alade, why did you not come to the party?'

'Why didn't I come to the party? But I've already told you, Glor. Just why —'

'Mr Alade Moses,' she cut him short. 'You can kid your political colleagues and Ministry of Works staff. But you cannot kid me, Mr Minister of State.'

'What exactly are you up to?' he asked, hesitating before entering the car parked under the mango tree near the three storey block of flats.

'You know what I mean all right. I thought the quarrel between you and Chief Franco-John is over.'

'And who told you it is not?'

'You think I'm a fool, with eyes that cannot see? What d'you take me for?'

'Oh Glor. You bother your head about things that are really no concern of yours. And half the time you come out with wild guesses that land miles away from the mark.'

'Matters that are no concern of mine. Matters which engage your attention and prey on your mind so much that you have no time to devote to me. I suppose I really have no right to talk to you like this. I know it is Bose who should —'

'Glor, please. For heaven's sake, please.'

'You think I'm just a piece of wood without any feeling. You cannot even trust me to look after your interest,' she sobbed. 'Alade you really must accept the way the Elders settled the quarrel. You cannot afford to quarrel long with Franco. He – will – des – troy you —'

On the way to the Premier's Lodge he drove rather absent-mindedly. He was worried that Gloria was worried about him. It was true that he had deliberately kept away from Franco-John's party for the Jordarmenian Ambassador because he had been frightened by certain proposals which the Ambassador had discussed with the Prime Minister, Franco-John and himself earlier on the day of the party. He had been so frightened about the possible repercussions that he had pretended to be unwell in the evening. Unfortunately the Director of Public Works had given a different reason for his absence at the party. Now Gloria had seen the inconsistency in his story and that of his Director.

Up till then he had resisted the temptation to tell Gloria the details of the oath swearing ritual in the bedroom at the Premier's Lodge the day the Elders settled the differences between him and Franco-John. Even now, several weeks after, the whole thing still looked to him like a dream – the medico Prime Minister taking some blood with a syringe first from a vein in Franco-John's left forearm and then some from his own and emptying the contents into a white enamel dish already half filled with water. He saw dimly his relation Chief Odole saying some incantation, after which he first drank of the concoction himself. Perhaps that was to show that he was not poisoning the principal characters in the ceremony – if it was poison he was offering, then the poison would first affect him himself. He remembered how Chief Odole had offered the dish to Franco-John next and how Franco-John had not hesitated to take a good draught of it. And then how he had followed suit, taking care to hide his fear as he did not want it said that he was a coward. No. Gloria or any other woman must not know this thing. Nor any man for that matter, save Chief Odole, the Prime Minister, and the two other Elders who had been the principal witnesses at the ceremony.

Several cars in the tarmac drive at the Premier's Lodge indicated that at this late hour the Prime Minister's day was far from coming to an end. The Principal Private Secretary told him as soon as he had finished parking his car that the Prime Minister would see him after he had finished with a paramount ruler who had been given a seven days' ultimatum by his subjects within which to abdicate his throne. While he waited his turn Moses flirted with the plump daughter of the Prime Minister, who was known to be the plaything of all the Ministers and V.I.P.'s in Victoria.

When Moses was eventually admitted into the air-conditioned study he was surprised to see that Chief Chris Band-Ogun looked as fresh as if he was just starting his first official appointment of the day. On the contrary Moses knew that the head of government's day started as early as 5.30 in the morning, when he dealt with a few party elders before a break for bath and breakfast, then another two hours of interviews before going to the office in Exco Chambers. On a typical Cabinet day he would be at the Cabinet meeting till late in the evening. Then back home after a rushed dinner he would continue his interviews in the study.

'Ah, Minister, glad to see you looking so fine after the day's hard work,' he said, offering Moses his hand without getting up from behind the massive mahogany desk.

'Thank you very much, sir. Glad to see you looking fit and fine in spite of the many hours of interviews you've been having today.'

'Thank you, Minister. I'm really quite well now. Nothing really wrong with me. All I need is to keep close to the Elders.'

'Yes, sir.'

'Yes. And to imbibe from their school something of the wisdom of our fathers. Something we must revive, my dear Minister, African super-science, erroneously called fetish and juju. Our independent nation will yet lead all Africa in the development of this branch of study that will one day place the African on the map of world knowledge.'

'Yes, sir,' Moses muttered. He wondered how to take the P.M.'s flight of imagination. Was this just a personal idiosyncrasy – or was the head of government going queer?

'Pity about all this bother about the libel case. Franco tells me something went wrong somewhere. He assures me the judgement will be reversed in the Supreme Court. You look somewhat sceptical, Minister?'

'Not that I'm sceptical, sir. But how can anyone outside say which way a court case will go – unless, unless one is really fixing the case.'

'Nothing of the sort, Mr Minister. The purity of the Judiciary must be the one thing we must preserve in this new nation,' the Prime Minister declared. 'Have a cigar.'

'Quite, sir. I'm not in the least suggesting anything fishy. But I fail to see the wisdom in Franco-John's or anyone else's assurances. He first told us we would win the case in the High Court.'

'And we lost it. But look, Minister. He's a lawyer. You are not. I'm not. The way of the lawyers, like their language, is like the peace of God. It passeth all understanding.' After he had held the lighter to his visitor's cigar, he continued. 'Look, Minister, we have committed to Franco's plate all legal matters. He is an experienced lawyer. And he knows the legal boys well. We must abide by his advice in these matters.'

'Yes, sir. And of course the election petition case too. He told me yesterday that the case is now properly in court and that we must prepare our defence.'

'Ah, yes, I heard about that too. Again we must leave this to Franco and the law boys. They tell me that Dauda and his boys don't have a chance.'

'So I hear too.'

'Look, Minister, I want you to leave the lawyers to handle these law-suits. What I really want you to do now is to give more attention to the things going on in your Ministry. You know the proposals of the Jordarmenian Ambassador. Franco thinks that they require much study. Minister, I want you to work more closely with Franco on these proposals.'

Moses was silent for some time.

'Well, Minister?'

'Please sir, I really beg for a transfer to Education, sir.'

'Education, now? Impossible, Minister.'

'But sir, I'm sure I'll be more able to make an intelligent contribution to our activities in education. It is the one area in which I'm knowledgeable. In Works, I'm really a fish out of water. In any case, something tells me that the proposals of the Jordarmenian Ambassador will lead to trouble and disaster. Please sir —'

'Minister, you surprise me. I thought we'd settled this question before. To remove any doubts on the subject, Moses, you remain in Works.'

'Is that final, sir.'

'I'm afraid that is final, Minister.'

The telephone rang. While the Prime Minister spoke to the voice at the other end of the line Moses reviewed the unfortunate situation he was in. He did not like the Prime Minister's iron hand and unsympathetic attitude. But he knew the Prime Minister had the backing of his kinsman Chief Odole and of the Newtown Improvement Union.

'Oh don't think I'm a dictator in this matter, Minister. But concede to me two advantages. Age and intuition. I know what I want done. And I know my team. Believe me, you are the best man for Works.'

'Yes, sir. But, but – the decision about State College. I just don't have the heart to carry that out. I can't face Geoff Shepherd to tell him that the building project is off.'

'You don't have to. The civil servants will tell him that.'

'But he will know that I did it. The Old Boys of State College will never forgive me. They will —'

'My dear Minister, the abandoning of the State College project is a decision of Cabinet for which the Cabinet has collective responsibility. Nothing to do with any individual Minister of State. Well, Minister?'

Moses smiled. He saw now that he had lost the battle.

Fourteen

$\diamond$

JOHN HARRINGTON read the letter in the file almost
unbelievingly. He turned the page over and re-read the
minute: 'DPW, Letter overleaf for your information and
necessary action. You are requested to confirm that you
have brought to the notice of the appropriate officers the
contents of this letter. The Principal Accountant has
instructions not to accept any expenditure against Head 701
Subhead 23 Item 7.' Here followed a signature which he
could not recognize. But he knew that it was the new Senior
Assistant Secretary. He wondered why information of this
importance should get to him through a minute (dated three
days before) from an officer of the status of an S.A.S. He
sighed at this reflection of the rapidly sinking efficiency of
the civil service. Why, when the expatriate Permanent
Secretary was there, he would have brought the letter
by hand and they would have discussed it over a cup of
tea.

He picked up his telephone and dialled a number. 'Jean?
Who's that? What? Isn't that the office of the Director of
Education? It is? Well, let me speak to his Secretary. What?
Kindly speak up, I can't hear you. You are the Secretary,
you say? Where's Mrs Jean Taylor then? – Oh, is that you
Derek? What the hell is going on in your office? An

Afromacolese Secretary, d'you say? I see. I see. In my own office? No. I still have June Jacoby here, thank God – Hello, Hello – HELLO!' He banged the receiver in fury. The telephone had suddenly gone dead in the middle of the conversation.

A few minutes later he was in the office of the Director of Education. 'Who's she?' he asked after shutting the door separating the office of the Director from that of his Secretary. In times past he would have stopped to have a flirting chat with the plump Jean Taylor.

'My new Secretary, John,' McDonald said, wearily. He waved him into a chair. In answer to the unspoken question posed by John Harrington's raised eyebrow, McDonald said that the Secretary to the Prime Minister had called him to a meeting earlier that day and told him that a policy decision had been taken by Government to attach qualified Afromacolese stenographers as Secretaries to important Ministries and that the girl whose name he could not even attempt to pronounce had been posted to his.

'That one – a qualified stenographer?'

'So I'm told, John,' McDonald sighed. 'Indeed she holds a degree from some American University.'

After a pause, John Harrington asked: 'And what's happened to Jean?'

'Jean? I believe she's being posted to the Treasury Training School.'

'Ah, they still trust her to do even that? Isn't that post covered by their new policy of Afromacolization? No security involved? My God!'

'I don't know, John. I don't know anything about anything these days. Certainly nothing about education, anyway.' McDonald showed in every inch of his five feet ten inches a disappointed man.

After some time, Harrington said: 'I fear I have bad news for you, Derek; quite bad . . .'

'What's it this time? I'm past worrying about anything.'

'Read this,' he said, opening the file he had brought with him at the page containing the letter from the Treasury. He placed the file on the desk before his companion.

'What!' Derek McDonald exclaimed. 'The State College project off?'

'Shelved indefinitely.'

'Shelved indefinitely – why?'

'Why? It's there in the letter. Economy drive.'

'Economy drive! But, but the contract has been signed. They cannot do that, can they?'

'But they are the Government.'

'So?'

'Government can do anything.'

After some pause, McDonald said: 'But the contractors will sue them. They can't get away with it. Oh dear, dear. Geoffrey Shepherd. This will kill Geoff.'

The intercom rang.

'McDonald. Who? I beg your pardon? I'm so sorry Mrs – er – but can you possibly say that again? Oh I see. Mr Stanfield. He's our Permanent Secretary. Not Mr Stanfield? Perhaps if you say that more slowly, I'm sure I can understand you. Oh, yes, Mrs – er. I think that will be much better. Please come in. What? you mean the Director of Public Works? Oh come in, I'm sure he'd love to see a pretty lady too.'

'Your new Secretary?' Harrington asked.

'God, my new Secretary,' McDonald sighed as he replaced the receiver. 'Couldn't hear a single thing she said. She's coming in,' he warned as they heard the knocking on the door.

'Come in.'

She came in, then hesitated after closing the door behind her.

'Come right in Mrs – er —'

'Mrs Ogun.'

'John, meet my new secretary Mrs O-gunn. Mr Harrington is the Director of Public Works, Mrs O-gunn.'

'I'm pleased to know you, sir,' she said, exhibiting what struck Harrington as a particularly good set of teeth even among Africans. African girls were usually not tall – something to do with malnutrition and the drinking of disease carrying water in the most important years of growth. But this one was tall and graceful – Harrington had not noticed that when he first went past her in her own room before getting to McDonald's. Of course then she was sitting on the stool – Jean's stool. And he was angry and prejudiced against her.

'Do you come from London, sir?' Lola asked, facing Harrington in a way that surprised both men.

'What, me, London?' Harrington laughed.

'I was in London for six months,' she said, again looking at Harrington, this time in a way that aroused in him a feeling that surprised him himself.

'No, I don't come from London. My people come from the West of England. I went to school in the Midlands. Fact is we have so few relations left in England now we really have no home there. You like London?'

'Well, yes and no,' she said, smiling confidently. 'Not as much as the United States.'

'You were in the States, then, Mrs – er?'

'Yes. After I spent six months in London I went to the United States. There I did my degree in Office Management: Principle and Practice.'

'I see, I see,' Harrington said, looking at her interestingly. It was not immediately apparent to see what he professed to see.

'You did not like the cold, I'm sure?' he asked.

'Not a bit,' she laughed.

'Ah, even we ourselves don't like it, Mrs – er.'

'Mrs Ogun. Lola Ogun,' again she smiled at Harrington.

'Ah, Laura, may I? Not Laura? Lolla, good.'

She blushed yes. Who said African girls don't blush? The feeling in Harrington mounted. He thought he'd finished with this sort of thing. He'd had his fun with African girls in his junior days in the service, when he felt the need for female companionship after the doctor had ordered Bessie back home for a delicate operation early in their third tour. He'd carried on for the next three tours with a particularly understanding girl from the East who satisfied his desires such as they were and demanded not much in return.

'Now Lola, who was it that left a message for me?' McDonald asked.

'Mr Garfield, sir.'

'Garfield, of course. From the United Africa Enterprises.'

'Yes, sir. His telephone is 20647.'

'2034-'

'647, sir.'

'20647, thank you, Laura,' McDonald said looking up from the pad on which he scribbled the number.

'Lola, sir, not Laura,' she corrected him giggling. 'L-o-l-a, Lola,' she spelt it out for them.

'Ah, Lola, I'm so sorry, so very sorry.'

The telephone rang.

'That must be Garfield now,' McDonald said, lifting the receiver. 'McDonald. Yes, Director of Education. Yes, this is McDonald, Director of Education. You want – Laura? Kindly speak up – I think this telephone is bad. My secretary is not Laura? Yes, Mrs O-gunn. Who d'you say is speaking? I see sir. I'll call her to the telephone, Minister.'

After he had handed the receiver to her he said to his companion: 'John, come to the conference room and see for yourself the population density on the map. You will then appreciate the problem we are up against.'

In the conference room Harrington asked: 'Which Minister was that, Derek?'

'Which Minister was that, d'you ask? How would I know? There are seventeen of them now,' he said wearily.

'No. Twenty-one. The number has risen to twenty-one. Four new ones were sworn in at Government House this morning.'

'I see. The fellow who spoke just now mentioned a Ministry. The portfolio title was completely strange to me. I'm sure I'm a very old man now. Incidentally that was the third Minister of State to ring Laura this morning.'

'Lola, not Laura,' Harrington corrected.

Lola knocked the door and came into the conference room.

'I've finished on the telephone, sir.'

'Oh, thank you, Laura – Lola, I'm sorry.'

'And I want to apologise to you. I'm sorry about people phoning me on your direct line. I don't know who gave them the number.'

'Oh no, Laura. Don't bother about that.'

'I'm sure it's the Prime Minister's Office who told them that I've been transferred to this office.'

'And of course they can look it up in the telephone directory,' Harrington said as Lola's slim figure disappeared through the door.

Harrington scanned the pages of the latest copy of *The Times* of London on McDonald's desk while the latter read through the minute about the State College project once more.

'John, do you know something?'

Harrington looked up.

'That minute is dated March 15th. Do you see that?'

'Yes?'

'You remember the date of the party of the Minister of Agriculture?'

'No. Why?'

'March 6th, Friday,' he read out from an invitation card which he sorted out from a pile in the third drawer of his desk. 'And the Jordarmenian Ambassador was at the party.'

'The contemptible little man,' Harrington said between his teeth.

'The contemptible little man. This minute is dated nine days after the party for the Jordarmenian Ambassador. There was a Cabinet meeting on March 12th. We know that as a matter of fact. And any amount of party Caucuses in between. Party Caucuses. These really are where they hatch their diabolical policies and plans.'

'You think the Jordarmenian Ambassador attended their political party meetings?'

'I don't think he would do his dirty business so openly. But I'm convinced that this thing has something to do with the visit of your friend from Jordarmenia. We must watch out for more trouble, John. Everywhere they've been in the developing countries they've dazzled the leaders of the emerging nations with their own success in nation building – their triumph over cruel nature in the desert wastes of their own homeland.'

'A spectacular success they have achieved, the devils. How they did it is still a miracle.'

'Dedication; that's the secret of their success. The will to live as a nation that can be identified with a territory of their own, instead of a people that form hated and persecuted minorities in all the big nations of the world. Stanfield told me on his return from his fortnight's visit to Jordarmenia last May that he had never seen a people more dedicated and more hardworking than these people in their country. You see their women, completely unconscious of their sex in the physical work they do. From Stanfield's account, and from what I've read in books, no one can have anything but admiration for the chaps in their own country. The tragedy of course is that what they do in these developing countries is another matter. My God, how they burrow their way into the hearts and minds of the leaders of these emergent nations and suck out the blood from their economy.'

'Oh yes?'

'From accounts I've read of their activities, they are terrible, John. They sell to the gullible African leaders the highly marketable stories of our neglect and exploitation in our former overseas territories'

'Damn it all, man. What do they have to say about the Spanish and the Portuguese. And about the French and the Belgians?'

'Don't get me wrong, John. We are not alone in condemming these newly-won friends of the African. No, you cannot accuse the Jordarmenians of discriminating against the British in that respect. They've lined up every nation that has had anything to do with Africa and the Americas since Columbus first sailed westward in the fifteenth century and Mungo Park jumped into the Niger at Bussa to escape being eaten by half-naked cannibals on the bank.'

After a pause McDonald concluded: 'After succeeding in worming their way into the confidence of the political leaders of the people, the Jordarmenians lure them into forming corrupt associations with them in which they suck the economic blood of these nations to the point of incurable economic anaemia. The tragedy is complicated by the dilemma we are in. We have been so badly maligned by both the leaders and their new friends that we are no longer in a position to warn them of the dangers ahead of them. You tell an Afromacolese politician of State not to hold a 230-volt live wire. His first reaction will be to hold it – he does not believe any Englishman can give an advice that is genuine.

'What they are doing now is terrible. The impact on all

of us involved in the tragedy is tremendous. But both they and their actions will soon pale into insignificance. Their country and their people will outlive the whole lot of them. And it is the future governments that will be saddled with responsibility for clearing the muck of the misgovernment of today.'

Fifteen

---◇---

MOSES was sincerely sorry and embarrassed about the decision to cancel the State College project. Apart from a number of old boys of State College in important positions in the civil service and in private business, he knew that the decision would annoy his friend Geoffrey Shepherd very much.

It did. McDonald, the Director of Education, had guessed that Shepherd might decide to resign his appointment but hoped that sanity would prevail and that he would be persuaded to remain at his job.

McDonald sighed when the official O.H.M.S. envelope containing Shepherd's letter of resignation came to his desk. He decided not to contact him immediately. He rang up the First Secretary at the British High Commission to tell him to contact the High Commissioner, who was then on a tour of the provinces. He would himself seek the advice of Harrington, the only other Britisher of experience and maturity. A very delicate matter, this case of Shepherd's. He cursed Moses and the whole host of Afromacolese Cabinet Ministers who had precipitated the crisis.

The following day Geoffrey Shepherd called to see him in his office at headquarters.

'I'm glad you've come, Geoff. This thing must have been

very trying for you, I know. We're all passing through trying times.'

Geoff Shepherd sat down without a comment. He took a cigarette from the case McDonald held to him.

'I hope you've now slept over this unpleasant matter of your resignation – and changed your mind?'

'I have slept over the matter,' Shepherd said slowly.

McDonald looked up, hope showing in his pallid face. He said just one word: 'Yes?' Into that one word he packed a wealth of meaning.

'Yes, I have changed my mind.'

'Oh, I'm so glad, Geoff,' the older man sighed, visibly moved. 'To throw away such a splendid career because of these – er – experimenters in parliamentary government. Why, they will make many more mistakes before they find their feet, which they eventually will. They are like little children playing with a giant toy. They have not yet mastered its intricacies.'

He noticed that his visitor did not show much enthusiasm for his philosophy. He got up and went to the safe at the corner of the room. He proceeded religiously to open it with a key out of a bunch which hung from a hook attached to the belt of his outsize khaki shorts. He brought out a green file marked 'G. F. Shepherd'. He locked the safe and went back to his seat. He opened the file and began to read to himself a sheet in it. Shepherd recognised his letter of resignation. He noticed that while the thing was in his confidential file it had in fact not been properly filed: it had not been strung through and page numbered. It was obvious McDonald was expecting that he would be persuaded to withdraw it.

'You will take this back then, Geoff? I will phone immediately to the British High Commissioner that you have changed your mind. He'd shown much concern about you, Geoff.'

'I've decided to stay on. But nothing to do with the

reasons that you and the others put forward. Oh, I appreciate the things people say all right. It's just so difficult to make people see my point of view.'

It had been difficult to make McDonald and the few senior expatriate officers left in the service of the Government see why a colonial civil servant of Geoffrey Frederick Shepherd's seniority and prospects should throw away an excellent career and lose all his retirement benefits in protest against the blunders of an all-African government cabinet. Why, London could transfer him immediately to one of the East African territories. The wind of nationalism which in Afromacoland had reached hurricane proportions was there just beginning to be felt as a gentle breeze. McDonald reviewed all this in his mind. But reopening the argument with Shepherd was unnecessary, indeed dangerous. He might change his mind again. He was so much emotionally strung up.

'The Minister of Works came to see me yesterday,' Shepherd said reflectively.

'Ah, the Minister of Works. Ex-schoolmaster turned politician. I thought they said that he at least has brains. Honest too, they said. About the only one of the lot one could so describe. Apparently he too has been behaving true to type.'

'I am afraid you are wrong there, sir. A most able man, Alade Moses. Combines a high sense of duty with unimpeachable character. A perfect gentleman.'

'Indeed?'

'Yes. Most distressed about the activities of his colleagues in the Cabinet. He's a very sad man.'

'Indeed. But if this is true why doesn't he do the obvious thing?'

'Clear out?'

'Why not – what would you do in similar circumstances? It's the one and only way out of the mess. How he ever got mixed up in the racket in the first place is difficult to understand in a man of his reputation. Look here, Geoff, if this man is all this good, talk to him. Try and drive some sanity into his head. And see if we cannot get back the State College project.'

Shepherd shook his head sadly.

'I see. I suppose your friend and his colleagues are already too far committed to the Jordarmenians.'

'The Jordarmenians?'

'Yes, the Jordarmenians. Did your friend not trust you enough to confide this to you?,' McDonald said in obvious contempt of Moses.

Shepherd looked at the older man for a long time. Then he said slowly: 'I'd rather not discuss this with you, sir. I'm sure you will understand my position.'

'I'm sure I understand your position. I'm glad you have decided to withdraw your resignation, Geoff. This is what concerns me. Stay on. I'm sure your friend will need you to advise him in the breakers ahead. I think the problems we've seen so far will pale into insignificance when we have the Jordarmenians properly entrenched among us. And, Geoff, if at any time you want a change of territory, just let me know. I have forwarded your particulars to London.'

Late in the night, Norman Bruce called to see Shepherd. He was the Chief Accountant of the United Africa Enterprises. They had been in the same squadron in the R.A.F. and took part in the Battle of Britain.

'I'm glad you've changed your mind, Geoff. These chaps just aren't worth the bother.' He sipped his beer. He'd developed a round tummy on the riotous living and extra generous allowances that the commercial firms paid their employees in Afromacoland.

'The High Commission people have traced the whole thing to the visit of the Jordarmenian Ambassador. Nothing good ever comes out of them, the Jordarmenians. Take it from me, real trouble is coming. Our chaps in London are keeping a close watch on the situation.'

Shepherd wondered how Bruce's prediction and assessment of the situation tallied with McDonald's. He nodded his head in understanding as he traced both to the original source of information – the local British intelligence.

'You would think that chaps like your friend Alad would put the brake on the excesses of his colleagues. Frankly speaking I'm disappointed in the chap. The fellow is as much a rogue as the others —'

'Norman, you probably don't understand the situation he's in.'

'The situation he's in! Just why is he in that situation, that's what I'd like to know; just why isn't he at the headmaster's desk at Newtown? That's what every reasonable person wants to know. Chap sent abroad by his community to be equipped with the proper tools for managing their community school on his return. Think of the way the chaps raised the funds – I saw them doing it during one of my visits to our Newtown Stores.' Here he drummed with his thumb on his tummy. 'They taxed themselves – pounds, shillings, and even sixpences from the old mammies selling oranges. Never seen such enthusiasm, such belief in a cause in all my nine years on the Coast. But what does our friend do the moment he gets back from Britain? Lured away by the glistening splendour of the life of a Minister of State from the austere, less romantic life of a schoolmaster. For all he cares the school in the bush can revert back to bush – as surely it will. And his community, why, what does he care about his community now?'

'Norman, I wish you would be less severe on Alade. You . . .'

'I really am sorry, Geoff. Perhaps I shouldn't be saying all this now. After all what matters is that you have now decided not to allow this act of insanity on the part of Alade

and his colleagues to make you throw up a splendid career.'
After another sip of his beer, he asked, his face creasing in
genuine puzzlement: 'But I'm sorry, Geoff, I still can't get
it. Just how has he convinced you about the need to
abandon the school project?'

'Remember he's not the Minister of Education.'

'No. But then there's something like collective responsibility in the whole Cabinet. Besides your Alade knows more
about education than the whole lot of them put together.'

'You see, Alade explained to me certain things which only
those who know him well can understand.'

'How he ever went into politics in the first instance – did
he explain that? I'm sure the thousands of Newtown men
and women who contributed their pounds and shillings –
and their pennies – would like to know that.'

After thoughtfully lighting a cigarette and inhaling a
sizeable quantity of smoke, Shepherd said: 'This will
surprise you. But those very people of Newtown persuaded
Alade Moses to go into politics.'

'How do you mean?'

'That same community that sent him to England that he
might come back to run their community school. It was
they who pushed him into politics. You no doubt have
heard that he was in Britain on a British Council trip when
his people nominated him and practically pushed him into
Parliament before informing him. You see he was the only
one in Newtown whose education was higher than that of
the rival candidate from a little town next door but belonging
to the same constituency. Something to do with these petty
inter-town, inter-village jealousies and rivalries.'

'Of course these are quite fierce, I know.'

'Difficult for us to understand these things. But to the
African they are real, very real. No doubt something going
back to the inter-tribal war days, when neighbouring
villages raided each other and carried away the able-bodied

men and women, and children to be sold to the traders on the Coast —'

'Or slaughtered as human sacrifices to their gods – my God!'

'In any case, Alade won the election quite easily. He was appointed a Minister of State. By so doing, he has placed his community on the map. Which to them was more important than the community school.'

After Bruce had refilled his glass he said: 'I see you are much devoted to this chap Alade. I imagine you can influence him. Make him see reason. Stay on, for your own sake, and his. You don't win a battle by running away at the sight of the enemy.'

'Alade's very argument, Norman. Why, when I asked him at the beginning of it all why he was going to get mixed up with the all sorts and conditions of people that would become his associates in politics he told me something that I've always remembered about him. "If you leave politics to the professional letter-writers and semi-literate men who live on the ignorance and misfortune of the masses, how can you ever expect the country to be properly administered?"'

'There's something in that, I daresay,' Bruce said, thoughtfully.

'Of course there is. The important business of lawmaking requires that each of these new legislative houses in the developing nations of Africa must include a few Alade Moseses to raise the quality of their deliberations and the integrity of their governments. Alade here believes that with half a dozen like himself this could be done in the Government of Afromacoland.'

Sixteen

◇

AFTER the meeting with the Prime Minister Alade Moses had decided that he had to make the best of a bad job. He managed to persuade himself, though without real conviction, that the State College project affair was as the Prime Minister had argued, something decided by the whole Cabinet for which he as the Minister of Works should feel no more responsible than the Minister of Agriculture or the carefree Minister of Local Government. He would stop worrying himself about the thing. He would settle down to do the more positive, more rewarding duties in his Ministry. He would take the rough with the smooth. In the end he would pile up a sufficiently high number of marks on the credit side to wipe his slate of stewardship clean of this very bad mark.

But he was not allowed to settle down long enough to test his new theory. One day in mid-morning he decided that he had seen enough party supporters, would-be contractors, and job-seekers for one day. He instructed his Private Secretary that he would see no one else. No one whatsoever, age, status, or sex regardless. He was just settling down to following the thread of argument in a rather voluminous report prepared by a Jordarmenian firm of experts on low-cost housing when his Secretary opened the door softly and took a few diffident steps towards his desk.

'If it is the lady I cannot see her,' he protested, irritation showing clearly in his voice. 'Or anyone else for that matter.'

'Not the lady, sir. It's Chief Odole,' the Secretary said, waiting for the reaction he knew was sure to come.

'Chief Odole!'

'Yes, sir. He came in just after you decided not to see any more people today.'

'I see,' Moses said somewhat absent-mindedly.

'Should I call him in, sir?'

'Yes. Call him in.'

Chief Odole tapped his way into his office with his umbrella. Moses, already on his feet, took a few steps towards his visitor. He girded round his middle the folds of his agbada. Then he prostrated before him, supporting one arm on the arm of a chair and the other on the floor. Before he became a Minister of State whenever he greeted the old man he went down flat on his tummy.

'Greetings to you, Father, this morning.'

'Greetings to you, my child. Do get up, get up, son of the tiger, son of the famous hunter of the Black Forest, the forest in which elephants abound in plenty – I've told you that when you greet me now you should not prostrate before me. I give you permission not to, my child.'

'But why should I not, Father? If even I become a Minister of State seven times over, I must give due respect to those who bore me.'

'My son, I've come to inquire after your health,' the old man said as he tried to balance his umbrella at the edge of the shining desk. 'And to discuss an important matter with you.'

'Thank you, sir. I am quite well.'

'This place is very cold. Is this how it is cold in England? I don't think this is good for your health.'

'It is the air-conditioner – that one in the wall . . .'

'That one making a noise like a motor-cycle engine?'

'Yes. It makes the room cool. When the room is cool, the brain is cool. Then one can work better.' Then he yawned.

'You are tired my son. You are working too hard.'

'There's much work to do, sir. It's amazing. I have to read through all these files. I have to attend so many meetings. Party meetings. Cabinet meetings. Then so many people come to see me . . .'

'I saw a large number of people in the office of your Secretary just now.'

'Yes, how can I see them all? They all want to see me. They all want me to give them jobs or to give their sons and brothers jobs. They all want to be contractors. I had to tell my secretary to send them away.'

'You must be careful. You cannot see them all. But you must be careful who you send away.'

'But it's just too much, Father. Too much. I'm fed up.'

'Our people from Ogbagba came to see me yesterday,' Chief Odole said in an undertone. He looked round the room as if to make sure that there were no others besides himself and Moses in the room. Then he continued. 'They want something very important from you. They want Government to tar the earth road between Ogbagba and Newtown. You know how important Ogbagba is. It was the original home of the two brothers that founded our own town. You know Gregory's father originally came from Ogbagba. And many other eminent men came from Ogbagba. Just now two Ogbagba boys are studying in the United Kingdom. When they come the Improvement Union wishes to hold the thanksgiving service for them in the church at Ogbagba. The new church building is nearing completion. It is necessary that members of the Union from Victoria and Newtown and their friends from abroad should be able to drive in their cars right up to Ogbagba that day.'

Moses had listened to the case in silence and surprise. Then he said: 'But I know that the Ogbagba people have been collecting money by voluntary subscriptions for this very road, Father.' That was true. He remembered then to his annoyance that the Improvement Union had diverted to the Ogbagba Road construction fund a sum of £200 which was sliced off the Newtown Grammar School Scholarship vote.

'Yes, and no,' the old man said, allowing a gulp of saliva to glide down his ancient throat. Moses waited for him to continue. He did: 'What the Ogbagba people collected together with what the Improvement Union gave them for the fund came to just over £700.'

'Well?'

'Then the District Engineer at Newtown spoilt the whole thing.'

'Mr George?'

'Yes. He told them that the road will cost several thousand pounds. The bridge over the Ogbagba River alone will cost, according to him, over £2000.'

'Yes, these engineering works cost a lot of money. That's what I've discovered here, Father.'

'That's why they've come to me. They can never collect all the money for the construction of the road. They want Government to construct it for them. You must do this for them.'

Moses contemplated his kinsman for some time. Then he said: 'The road is not a trunk road.'

The old man's face seemed to ask: 'Trunk road, what does that mean?'

'Trunk roads are the main roads which connect the big towns in the country. They are owned and maintained by Government. The road between Newtown and Ogbagba belongs to the Newtown District Council. They should reconstruct it. Besides, Government has no money now.'

Chief Odole looked distressed. He did not say anything for a while. When he did he said: 'My son, you must not talk

129

like this to the hearing of Ogbagba people. You must do the favour they ask of you. You will construct the road, you must construct it. Government must find the money. If you don't do it, we will never again be able to look our people in the face. How can we say we have a Minister son who cannot construct our road? Who will believe that?'

Moses went back home almost immediately after Chief Odole left him. More than ever he saw the hopelessness of his situation. He was convinced he would never be happy in this Ministry. Once more he cast a longing eye across to the portfolio of Education.

The following night he battled with a self-imposed assignment, the writing of a party policy speech on education. He would deliver the speech at the rally in Moyamba where the opposition were giving trouble. He would kill two birds with one stone: defend his State College project decision, and show the Prime Minister and the party hierarchy that he really ought to go to Education.

He smiled the smile of the satisfied as he wrote the last three words of the last sentence. He put the figure 3 at the top of the page. He had had to come back to that third sheet and rewrite it. His thoughts just weren't flowing properly when he was doing the draft the first time. The wound his action had inflicted on his friend Shepherd kept on coming to his mind again and again. A large number of cigarette ends in the ash-tray told the tale of the struggle going on in his mind.

He tore up the discarded original third sheet, crumpled it and threw it into the waste paper basket. He smoothed the creases in the second sheet and after sandwiching it between the first and the new third sheet, clipped the lot together.

'If our critics thought that our government – this government of our people by our people for our people – was going to build the superstructure of our great educational edifice on the shaky foundation left by our colonial masters, then let them think again. We tell them that we know better than to put new wine in old bottles. We will have nothing to do with any foundation that bears any element whatsoever of our unedifying past – a past that we must forget in double quick time.

'The missionaries of old – God rest their bones in their graves —' He looked up from the sheet he was reading. He remembered how he had started that sentence originally with the idea of condemning unreservedly the activities of missionaries. Then his conscience had interfered, reminding him of the kindness of the missionary doctor who, having cured him of a serious bout of malaria, had given him £3.10s. towards his examination fees for the Intermediate Bachelor of Arts, which he had passed as an external student of the University of London. This was why he watered his original idea down to: 'The missionaries of old – God rest their bones in their graves.' Then he remembered immediately that he was a nationalist, he was a politician. He was not an individual. While an individual Afromacolese could show his appreciation and gratefulness to an individual expatriate benefactor, there was no room for the expression of such sentiments in the speech of a Minister of State. He decided to continue the paragraph at a middle-of-the-road level: 'They meant well. They were kindly people, devoted to the cause of producing black missionaries and school masters, and the laymen – the rejects of their training colleges – who manned their many bookshops in which they sold the Holy Bible and the Book of Common Prayer – and Bunyan's *Pilgrims Progress*. To them the alpha and omega of education was the manufacture in their factories in the mission schools and training colleges of the men and women who would labour in the Lord's vineyard, preparing the mind of the African in this world for everlasting life in the world to come.

'Of these well meaning missionaries we can in all honesty

say: 'Father, forgive them for they know not what they do'. But if we of this age can forgive the missionaries for the sins they have committed against this nation, we of this age will never forgive the hirelings of the British imperialists for their efforts to throw spanners in the spokes of the wheel of our educational programme. Posterity will not forgive Abdul Dauda and his fellow fifth-columnists in our midst for the crime they are today perpetrating against our nation. When the day of reckoning comes, as surely it will, the God of Africa will visit the sins of Abdul Dauda and his gang of collaborators upon their children and their children's children unto the third and fourth generations.'

Abdul Dauda! The man was the bane of his political life. Why did Dauda pursue him so relentlessly? Why did he concentrate the venom of his powerful pen on him of all the members of the Cabinet? Dauda was reported to have admitted to a third party once that he secretly admired Alade Moses for his intellect, courage, and integrity and that he was aware of the fact that Franco-John was the scoundrel behind the nefarious activities of the Cabinet. But if Dauda was aware of this, and knew something about the theory of collective responsibility in parliamentary government, why should he continue to blame upon him all the ills of Government?

He sighed unhappily as the result of the libel case against Dauda flashed through his mind. The High Court had thrown out the case for some technical reason he could not understand. Some said it was due to the carelessness and negligence of the Q.C. barrister that the Party had engaged for him. He recalled that Franco-John had said categorically that it was because the Judge was in the pay of the Opposition and that the Government Party was sure to win the case on appeal. The indignity of losing a case in which one was the central figure, though not the footer of the bill for the expenses, was bad enough. The greater indignity of having approached the Minister of Home Affairs to use his influence with the Judge to interfere with the course of justice made him thoroughly ashamed. And what was worse than all this: the Opposition's use of the court judgement to attack him more viciously. He was apprehensive of the outcome of the election petition then pending in the same court which had just humiliated him. Since the Prime Minister told him that the attempt to unseat him from Parliament had failed due to a technical blunder by the Opposition, the latter had rectified their mistake and filed the motion afresh. In spite of the comforting assurances of the lawyers of the Government Party Moses knew that his case was bad. Still he hoped for the best. He proceeded with the speech he was drafting:

'Our detractors are after our blood because we decided in the interest of the many not to increase the privileges of the few. That in a land where a large number of children of school age have no schools to go to the luxuries enjoyed by the very few boys in the Government-owned State College should not be increased. That instead of spending the gigantic sum of £250,000 on new buildings for the education of only 230 boys, this amount should be spent on the expansion of primary education from which hundreds of thousands of boys will benefit.'

He read on: 'We shall restate our case. Our greatest asset as a nation is our human resources. We must develop the over forty million inhabitants of this country that in their turn they may develop the vast natural resources with which the good God of Africa has blessed our nation. We must invest all available funds in the education of all children of school age to the end that we may wipe out illiteracy in our country in one generation.

'They that want us to spend a quarter of a million pounds on new buildings for one single school pooh-pooh our intention to introduce universal primary education in our country. They say it is impossible to find the money for the building of the schools and the teachers that will teach in the many thousands of new schools that they estimate would be required. Yes, it truly would be impossible if we had to build every school for a quarter of a million pounds and if every teacher would have to be an honours degree man as the arm-chair experts of the Ministry of Education would have us believe. But this is precisely what this Government will not do. This Government is determined to abandon as an untenable anachronism the colonial policy of concentrating scarce resources on the over-luxurious education of a very small minority to the utter neglect of hundreds of thousands of other children. We in this Government condemn without reservation the importation into this country of the British public school system. The education of a handful of boys at an exorbitant cost to the taxpayers of a country who cannot find schools for their own children is untenable in a country the affairs of which are in the hands of nationalists like ourselves.'

What was wrong with that argument? Who except a fool would not plug for the training of a hundred boys instead of one if the same amount of money would do either? He remembered the argument of the loud-mouthed Secretary of the Old Boys Association of State College that Government was abandoning the State College project because of pressure from former schoolmasters now in important State and party positions, who had always been jealous of the financial care which the Government gave State College compared with the voluntary agencies, particularly the community school authorities, who attempted to achieve much with little or no resources. He had denied at the meeting of the Select Committee of the Cabinet that met the delegation of the Old Boys Association that a number of schoolmasters of voluntary agency schools had formed themselves into a clique for the purpose of fighting against the care that

Government appeared to be lavishing on State College while other schools were starving for funds and for trained teachers. But he knew that the allegation was correct. And more than that he knew that the decision to abandon the State College project was readily acceptable to a number of his colleagues for this reason even though the immediate cause of it was the proposals put forward by the Jordar-menian firm.

'We here and now declare war, total war, against the common enemy, illiteracy. Let each man be his brother's keeper in this mass movement against illiteracy. Let each one teach one – everyone that can read and write must teach another man to read and write. Let each man reach one with the message of hope and salvation and the light of knowl-edge. We shall teach the children and their fathers in their houses in the towns and in their huts in the villages. We shall teach them under the trees in the town squares and in the village squares.

'We appeal to all, irrespective of race or creed or political affiliation, to join in this holy crusade against illiteracy. In particular we stretch our hand of fellowship to the oppo-sition to join us in this struggle of a life-time for the redemption of our people from the shackles of illiteracy. This is a worth while struggle that cuts across the boundary of party politics. There is much we can achieve together: there is much honour that we can share together when the fight is over. But, with them, without them, and in spite of them, the fight will be fought till victory is won against illiteracy and against the vestiges of imperialism.'

Seventeen

———————◇———————

BUT Moses, poor boy, was destined to continue with the unwanted portfolio of Works. Once more he convinced himself that since everyone wanted him in that Ministry – everyone except himself – the most sensible thing to do was to settle down to study the problems of the Ministry and forget all about the portfolio of Education.

'Keep our secrets secret,' he chuckled to himself one morning in his bathroom. Quite an effective way of saying just what it said, Alade Moses thought after saying the new slogan to himself as he was completing his shaving. He had seen the new poster and the slogan only the day before. One up for the Ministry of Information. No doubt the product of some clever civil servant in the Ministry, an Assistant Senior Secretary or Senior Assistant Secretary, he could never remember the correct permutation of the words. Must be the former, for he recalled with a chuckle that Franco-John had said in desperation one day that the abbreviation ASS meant exactly what these allegedly highly paid senior administrative officers are – asses, without brains. Franco-John had said that the vast majority of civil servants were mediocre in ability, lacking in initiative – at least initiative of the right kind – and full of intrigue and hate for the constitutionally elected government of the nation. Moses did not agree with his Ministerial colleague all the way – he knew the Minister of Agriculture had his own selfish reasons for hating civil servants for their traditional bureaucracy and the worship of files. But it was of course true that in a service which had no reward for initiative, no punishment for lack of it, but ensured an annual increment for the chap who for a period of twelve months had not offended against General Orders and Financial Instructions, the two testaments of the service, such of the young men as had had any initiative whatsoever at the beginning of their civil service career had had it killed pretty thoroughly after two or three years of searching aged, dust-ridden files for missing correspondence.

People wondered why a university degree was necessary for appointment into the administrative service in view of the type of work the civil servants had to do. Three weeks before, the Cabinet had considered a memorandum from the Minister of Establishment explaining why Government must have only graduates with honours degrees in the Administrative Class. Moses knew it was the Minister of Education himself who had queried the need for such high standards in entrants to the service. He also knew that this was due to representations made to him and to nearly all his Cabinet colleagues by an influential party member whose son had been rejected by the Civil Service Commission on the grounds that he did not possess the qualifications for the post as specified in the scheme of service.

Keep our secrets secret! Again he thought that the author of it must have been one of the few who really did not belong in Franco-John's class of 'asses'. One with a mind for the beautiful. Who knew what a Churchill was wasting away in one of those offices in the Secretariat!

He was now dressing. He sighed at the knowledge that he had not kept the secret of the Cabinet secret. He remembered his discussions with Geoffrey Shepherd. A Minister of

State had told a civil servant things that he knew his colleagues in the Cabinet and in the Party would have objected to. He, an African Minister of State and a nationalist leader had told an English civil servant things that he knew ought not to have been said outside the Cabinet. He had violated his oath of secrecy. But he convinced himself that the circumstances were out of the ordinary and justified his actions. In any case he knew that most of his Cabinet colleagues were guilty of not keeping Cabinet secrets secret. Party Elders and other members outside the House were in possession of Cabinet secrets. And the Jordarmenian Ambassador was a veritable mine of Cabinet secrets. Then, too, Geoffrey Shepherd was not an ordinary English civil servant. His association with Shepherd in the last three years had resulted in such understanding and near perfect meeting of minds that the wall of race and colour between these two had been practically dissolved by their common pursuits of the objectives of the advancement of African education. The fellow had a better claim to his confidence than Franco-John and his other colleagues. The fellow had a reason to know why he, Alade Moses of proven integrity, was behaving the way he was behaving. Above all Shepherd ought to know why he his friend was party to a decision that affected State College, his only love, so adversely.

But that was all the Englishman was entitled to know, he thought, with a frown. He was not entitled to know the details of the oath administered to him and to Franco-John by one of the Party Elders when they had settled the quarrel between the two of them in the bedroom of the Prime Minister. That was a secret he must keep secret from anyone outside that inner circle of the most senior members of the Party.

His police orderly held open the door of the official Mercedes Benz 220S which he had been using since his own car was laid up three days before. As he climbed out of the car he checked the time on his gold wrist watch. Nine-twenty. Another one hour and forty minutes before the meeting of the Ministerial Committee on universal primary education. He climbed slowly, nearly absent-mindedly, the concrete steps leading to the first floor on which his offices and those of his Permanent Secretary were situated. He acknowledged with stiff nods the greetings of the clerks and messengers carrying files along the balcony. The Private Secretary was having an argument with a man in white kaftan robes who had refused to join the many other people wanting to see the Minister in the Waiting Room. Inside his own air-conditioned room, he removed his well laundered white lace agbada which he handed over to the orderly for disposal on one of the six brass hooks on a highly polished two by one mahogany piece on the wall. He walked across the soft carpet on the floor. That was good. Newly supplied by Kingsway Stores. Chosen by Gloria. He pressed the button on his buzzer. He yawned deep into the receiver.

'You want me to come in now, sir?'

'No, not yet. Who's that man?'

'He says his name is Coker, sir.'

Coker? Coker? He wondered. Who was Coker now? One of these sleek Victoria boys. He'd seen the face before, he was sure of that. No doubt some important Party contact man, the way he refused to stay in the waiting room.

'And what does he want?'

'Says he wants to see you, sir. He says he's from Mamma de Mamma, sir.'

Ah, yes. He remembered. Mamma de Mamma was the girl-friend of Franco-John, the Secretary of the strong market women's union of Afromacoland. Some said that hers was the hand that rocked the throne of government. Others said that in spite of all her intrigues and advances the Prime Minister did not think much of her. Moses remem-

bered that she had just come back from a fortnight's tour of
Jordarmenia as a guest of the women of Jordarmenia. Then
he remembered the Jordarmenian Ambassador, the im-
pending scholarship of Gloria to work in the Teaching
Hospital in the Jordarmenian capital. And he remembered
the deal!

'I'll see him in ten minutes.'

'Yes, sir.'

'Any other people to see me?'

'Yes, sir . . .'

'All right,' he said, regretting his silly question. Of course
there were many people to see him. Party members, looking
for patronage. Church members, looking for donations for
their church building. School leavers from Newtown looking for jobs in the Secretariat. And beautiful women, either
representing themselves or hired by building contractors
that they might find favour with the Minister of Works via
the bed of the Minister of Works.

'Any mail?'

'Yes, sir.'

Another silly question. Was there any day when there was
no mail? Was there any day when someone did not write
asking for a scholarship for his son? Was there a day when
a schoolboy did not write pleading with the Minister to pay
his school expenses since his father had died suddenly and
his mother had been in hospital as a result of a motor
accident? Was there a day when a zealous party member had
not written to report that some constituency men were in
the pay of the Opposition and passing on information to
that Party?

'Am I to bring in the mail, sir?'

'Ye-e-s,' he said slowly. 'Yes, in five minutes. Meanwhile,
get me the Principal Private Secretary to the Prime Minister.
Quite urgent. And after that . . .'

'Yes, sir?'

'After that —' he broke off in the middle of the sentence and exploded in a sneeze at the same time that he dropped the receiver.

Ten minutes later he started reading the letters brought to him in a file jacket by his Private Secretary who stood at right angles to him. His face contorted in a frown as he read the third of these letters. 'We the entire officers and members of the Freedom for All Party have decided today at a monster mass meeting to communicate to the Prime Minister and the entire Cabinet our final and irrevocable decision that the Honourable Minister of Works must transfer the District Engineer, Mr Theophilus George, from our District. Since the glorious day when our Party won the bloody General Election and it pleased God Almighty to entrust the affairs of this great nation into the able and safe hands of our godly Prime Minister and his God-fearing lieutenants in the Government, Mr Theophilus George has done everything to bring our Government to ridicule. He hates our Party and he does not hide this hatred. In spite of all gentlemanly approaches to him he has continued to treat the Party members in particular and the townspeople in general with insult and indignity.

'He has set aside the very important decision taken by the Executive of the Party at the Moyamba Conference that only Party supporters should in future be awarded government contracts. This civil servant has said openly that he does not believe in the principle that those who serve at the altar should eat the crumbs that fall from the altar. He has said openly that he does not care about the Minister of Works and that the only person that has authority over him and whose instructions he can obey is the Director of Public Works, who is an expatriate.

'This gentleman persecutes and menaces officers of his Department whose only offence is their loyalty to our Party. He is just now conspiring with his expatriate boss in the

Secretariat to transfer the Head Road Overseer from this District just because he does not agree with him. This Road Overseer has been in this station for seventeen years and is responsible for the construction of all the good roads in the District. He has endeared himself to all and sundry in the District and his transfer from here will be a great calamity to the town and to the Party.

'Theophilus George is too full of his own importance and too keen on working for his friends in the Opposition. We are in possession of incontrovertible evidence that he is in the pay of the Opposition. Our security men have got all the evidence carefully documented. We therefore call on Government to remove immediately this satanic civil servant before he does more damage to the cause of our great Party. Freedom now . . .'

Oh dear oh dear! The things that some people would commit to paper! Of course the Private Secretary had read it. He wondered how much the fellow was to be trusted. He knew that he had been screened by the Secretary to the Prime Minister. Private Secretaries to Ministers were supposed to be acceptable to the Ministers before they were posted to the Ministries. The appointment of this particular one had been cleared with him. Other Ministers insisted on their Private Secretaries coming from their own towns – for a hundred per cent reliability. He had not gone this far with his own Private Secretary. But he had got the assurance from the Prime Minister's Secretary that the chap was quite safe with political secrets.

But the problem was not the private secretary. It was the several others who inevitably saw these papers. He remembered how Franco-John had once said that the messenger knew more State secrets than the Prime Minister. Then he reflected unhappily at the decision at the Party Executive that government contracts should be awarded only to Party supporters. He had opposed it both from conviction and from the knowledge that he would have the greatest difficulty getting the thing past his own officials. He remembered this was one of the many things that cropped up when the Elders went into the cause of the trouble between him and Franco-John. Even though he had agreed to carry out this Party directive by issuing the necessary instructions to his officials via his Permanent Secretary he just hadn't seen his way clear to doing it. 'Mr Harrington, just a little matter in which I need your co-operation. I hardly know how to begin . . .' That was just the problem. He hardly knew how to begin it. Just how did one say to a civil servant that contracts for government works financed from public funds should not be given out to the men who by knowledge, experience, and financial standing were most suitable for them but that they should be given to the shoemakers, the barbers, and the unattached women with painted lips, the new class of society known as Party supporters?

What now was he to do?

Eighteen

THEOPHILUS GEORGE, District Engineer of Newtown, called to see the Director of Public Works on what to him was a very important matter. The lean expatriate secretary told him that John Harrington had been called away suddenly to the Premier's Lodge but he had just telephoned from there that she was to get some papers ready for him for an important meeting at the Jordarmenian Embassy at eleven. That meant that the Director would call in the office before going to the Jordarmenian Embassy, she said. She could not tell, however, if he would be able to see him for a few moments in between the two appointments.

'But you fixed this 10.30 appointment for me to see Mr Harrington, Miss Jacoby,' George protested.

'I'm so sorry, Mr George, but Mr Harrington didn't know that he would be called out to the Premier's Lodge.'

'I see,' George said tersely.

'As I say, he will be here for a few minutes. Maybe he will decide to see you then.'

'Thank you, Miss Jacoby. I'll wait.'

She smiled him into one of the two easy chairs in the room. 'Coffee, Mr George?'

'No, thank you.'

George did not like June Jacoby and did not pretend to

like her. Miss Jacoby did not like George but pretended to like him. George was tipped by all to be the first African Director of Public Works. While most of the English community in Victoria tried to fraternize with him George felt that they did not really like him and did not wish him well. He thought June Jacoby was typical of them.

'There he comes now,' she announced smiling as she recognized the peculiar pounding of the heavy shoes of her boss on the concrete floor of the verandah.

'Ah Mr George,' Harrington said tiredly as he saw George on entering his secretary's room. 'I knew I was expecting you this morning. But I've been called away by the Prime Minister. And I'm off to another appointment at – er – the Jordarmenian Embasy. Can we not put off this appointment of yours till – er – Friday?'

'I would rather talk to you now, sir, if you don't mind.'

'All that urgent?' Harrington asked, disappointed, holding the handle of the door to his room. 'Well, come in then.'

Inside Harrington did two things simultaneously: with a paper knife he slit open an envelope marked 'Secret' and slid into his chair with great caution as if he must not hurt it. He read the contents of the single sheet from the envelope and for a moment appeared unaware of the presence of George. The latter coughed to correct the situation.

'Yes Mr George. All is well at Newtown, I take it?'

'No sir. All is not well in Newtown. And that's why I'm here.'

'Oh, what's the matter now? Surely things are going on according to the wishes of the people of Newtown?'

'I've just received this letter, sir, about the construction of the Newtown-Ogbagba Road. I do not understand it, sir. There is no vote for it.'

'Mr George, I wish you will not be too rigid in these matters. The Treasury has taken care of the financial side of the construction. The Minister wants the road done. And we do it. Well?'

'But this road is not even a trunk road. It isn't Government's responsibility at all.'

'Mr George, I wish you would leave what is Government's responsibility and what is not to the Treasury and this headquarters,' he said rather harshly. Then he continued, a little relaxed. 'Can't you see, young man, we are passing through hard times?'

'I'm going to be frank with you, sir. I'm rather worried about what's been going on in the last two months. Orders from headquarters about petty contracts in the field. Orders to stop vital work of maintenance of government roads and buildings because we have no funds. Now we are to embark upon the construction of Local Authority roads with government funds. Just what are we going to put forward as the economic justification for this road? I really can't understand why we are doing it.'

The Englishman's eyes were red. 'You want to know why we do what we do, young man? You want to know the economic justification for the little village roads that we now do, Mr George? Do not ask me. Ask him, the Honourable Alade Moses. Minister of Works. And I suppose you want to know the cost/benefit ratio too? Ask Chief Franco-John, Attorney General and Minister of Agriculture, the real power behind the throne of your government. D'you hear? Alade Moses. Franco-John. Chief Band-Ogun. They are my reasons for doing what I do . . . They are the economic justification, the cost/benefit ratio . . . And don't you ask me about the moral, young man. The pending by-election of your precious Minister – that's the moral, . . . oh dear, oh dear . . .' and the elderly man sobbed into his cupped hands.

George slipped out of the room, thoroughly embarrassed by the unfortunate scene he had witnessed. He decided that both his body and his mind needed cooling. So he drove to the 'Old Coaster's'. As he manœuvred his Opel Rekord in the badly designed drive of the Club he recognized Norman Bruce's old Citroen 1600 among the three cars parked at the Club. The United Africa Enterprises Accountant was the Honorary Treasurer of the Club.

'Ah, my friend Theo,' Norman Bruce cried from the bar. Holding up his glass of beer he said: 'Welcome to the Coaster's – and to civilization. From Newtown today?'

'Yes. Arrived in Victoria two hours ago. And departing Victoria another two hours.'

'Nonsense. Stay the night. Stay with me. The Missis is not in —'

'Which of them?' George asked mischievously.

'Ah,' Bruce sighed. 'Don't pretend to be good. But I haven't included bigamy in my list of crimes. My Mary is my Missis. Gone to Moyamba for the second burial of her great grandfather's uncle – some relationship like that.' He stroked his whiskers. He drummed with his left thumb on his tummy.

'Oh yes,' George said, sitting on the stool next to Bruce. 'Steward —'

'Forgive my carelessness, Theo. Steward, whisky and soda for the District Engineer of Newtown. Whisky and soda all right, Theo?'

'Beer. The coldest available.'

'Ah, Star then. Nothing like it.'

'Like Sammy Sparkle says: it is beer at its best,' George said after the departing steward.

'Look man, how did you get across the bridge that collapsed at Mile 16?' Bruce asked seriously.

'Culvert, not a bridge, man,' George corrected his companion.

'Culvert? Bridge or culvert, whichever you call it in engineering, fact is, it has paralysed traffic on this trunk road

147

for three days. A serious thing for my company. And for the economy of the country.'

'We've repaired it now,' George said, taking a good pull at his beer.

'You have? And traffic is back to normal?'

'Traffic is back to normal,' George said in a way indicating sensitiveness to criticism of his work.

'Look, this is no business of mine. But I can't help hearing what people say. They say that culvert was constructed only two months ago. Come to think about it, it is true I saw old Alhaji Musa mucking about the place about that time. Why in the name of Jesus did you ask that bloke to construct a bridge? He knows nothing about bridge construction or any kind of construction. He's only a barber.' Bruce laughed at the idea of the whole of the P.W.D. organization having been fooled by an ordinary barber.

'A barber?'

'Yes. My barber. And a bad one too,' Bruce said, again laughing at the idea of a barber taking the P.W.D. for a ride.

After a silence during which George topped up his beer, he said: 'We didn't give that job to your Musa man. We in Newtown knew nothing about it. Headquarters did.'

'It's true then what we hear. Political interference in technical and routine matters. Things must be pretty rotten for you, Theo.'

Rotten was an understatement. His mind raced through things that he had been going through during the last few months. Here he was, a professionally qualified engineer, the most senior African engineer in the Department, now being subjected to the humiliation of having petty contractors selected and petty contracts awarded at Headquarters in respect of works in his District. It was most amazing that Alade Moses, with whom he once shared the same lofty ideals for development and progress in Afromacoland, could

148

have done things like this. He sighed as the scene in Harrington's office came to his mind again.

'This Moses chap,' Bruce primed him. 'A decent fellow, honest and intelligent from all accounts. Geoffrey Shepherd swears by his name. I understand he went into politics with the idea of infusing clean blood into the damned thing.'

'So I too have heard,' George said, the sarcasm quite unhidden.

'But tell me man, what could be responsible for his rapid deterioration?'

'That's what all decent Afromacolese are wanting to know. And all interested in the future of Afromacoland. A suitable subject for a Ph.D. thesis in psychology.'

'Theo,' Bruce said, in the manner of someone about to introduce an important topic. He started refilling his companion's glass. 'They say it's true he wasn't properly elected in his constituency. In fact I hear there wasn't any election at all. You were in Newtown at the time. What really happened?'

'D'you know something, Norman, I've heard that story too. It is rumoured there was something defective about his nomination and the way he was declared unopposed. But to tell you the truth I lost interest in Alade Moses and everything about him right from the start.' George fidgeted with his glass.

'I see,' Bruce said, nodding his head.

'And isn't this matter what the law chaps call *sub judice*? We must watch out against being landed in the High Court for contempt. I am only a poor civil servant.' Then he remembered that Harrington had mentioned the by-election in his outburst. Had he known the result before the judgement? Good Lord.

'Of course,' Bruce laughed. George knew his companion was not satisfied with his explanation.

Theo rose to his feet and yawned. 'I think I must be going now,' he said.

'Me too,' Bruce said, his hand again on duty at his whiskers.

'Thanks for the drink, man.'

'You are welcome. Oh, steward, what's the damage?'

'Six and three, sah,' the steward said.

'Six shillings, three pence,' Bruce said as he drew out his wallet. 'One, two, three, four, five, six, seven,' he said slowly as he counted out the coins. 'And you can keep the change, Jeremiah.'

'Thank you sah,' the steward cried happily.

Theo George was about to slip the gear lever into number one when he suddenly changed his mind. He switched off the engine and got out of the car. He met his companion half way up the walk to the steps of the verandah.

'Look, Norman, you asked a short while ago how I was getting on with the old man. There's something I just cannot understand about Harrington, I must confess to you. Perhaps you can help me.'

'Oh yes?'

'Yes,' George said, as they took slow steps towards his car. 'You know I had a row with him today just before I came to the Club.'

'The devil you did!' Bruce said, interested.

'Indeed about the only reason why I came to the Club at all. To drown my anger in beer.'

'Good idea. But tell me what happened.'

Theo George appeared to debate in his mind for a minute the propriety of discussing an essentially civil service matter with a non-civil servant. But he eventually decided to get the load off his mind. 'I have recently been receiving from Headquarters a number of instructions for works which are clearly not the responsibility of Government. The construction of township roads which are the responsibility of the

Newtown Town Council, for instance. The construction of roads linking villages in the District. These roads have nothing to contribute whatsoever to the economy of the country.' After a short pause he continued: 'When I first came to the station I was impressed by the way the people constructed and maintained these village roads. Each family or household was taxed a certain amount according to the number of able-bodied males in it. The money was used for paying the labourers, usually from the villages too. The Newtown Improvement Union was very active in organizing these communal activities.'

'I hear they've done a great deal in this sort of way. In the days before Pax Britannica each household contributed not money but actual labour. Able-bodied members of the family worked for a week at a time on a road project.'

'Quite. But in the last few months the people appear to have stopped doing anything for themselves. They now say that as their own son is Minister of Works, Government must look after all the work of construction in their community.'

Norman Bruce nodded, again stroking his whiskers in understanding.

'But what beats me is this. If the people of Newtown didn't know what was their responsibility and what were their privileges, if Alade Moses had tasted power and got intoxicated and made dishonest by it, how does one explain the attitude of Harrington, the Director of Public Works? Just what has he got to lose by telling the truth – and standing by it?' George asked seriously contemplating his companion as if to say he knew he had the answer to his problem.

'He doesn't advise properly then?' Bruce asked, sitting on the bonnet of his car.

'Advise properly? Haven't you heard the things I've been saying? Issuing crazy instructions from Headquarters.

Registering barbers and tailors as road contractors and giving them culverts to construct?'

'Quite serious, I admit,' Bruce said, nodding his head in understanding.

'And when today I asked if he had considered the economic justification of the two roads he had asked us to start constructing in my district, you know what he did?'

'No,' Bruce said, expectantly.

'I can hardly believe it wasn't a dream,' George said, reflectively. 'The man just exploded, losing his temper completely. "The economic justification of the road construction, you ask me?" he cried. "Don't ask me, ask him, Alade Moses Esq., Minister of Works. He is the economic justification. Ask your government, your cabinet ministers, not me. They are the economic justification and the cost/benefit ratio of all the things we do."'

'He said that, really?'

Theo George nodded his head. 'I still find difficulty believing what happened. First the fellow losing his temper that way. Then why an Englishman should —'

'There's something you must know about old John Harrington. It's Bessie, his wife. You don't know her, do you?'

George shook his head.

'No, you couldn't have known her, come to think of it. She's an invalid in Dundee. Became a nervous wreck after her second tour with John. Her one consuming ambition is to see Harrington awarded the O.B.E.'

'Oh yes?' George said, hungry for the rest of the story.

'Each time the Honours List was published – Queen's Birthday and New Year Honours – John's name was missing, and Bessie's condition deteriorated, but she hung on to life, precariously. Harrington became dejected and disappointed for his own sake, but more for Bessie's. Each time Harrington went home on leave, each time Bessie sent him back to the battlefield in Africa, in quest of the O.B.E. It's become an obsession with them.'

'I see,' George nodded his head, understanding beginning to come to him.

'Harrington nearly died of a broken heart when on the last Birthday Honours List before Independence his name was missing again,' Bruce said, apparently sorry for the absent Harrington.

'I see now,' George said, again nodding his head.

'Now that the seat of power has shifted, it appears to me that John Harrington is now doing anything that will let him stay in favour with the new rulers. The man just cannot risk not getting the blessed thing next time.'

'I see it now. I'm sure I see it now,' George said, beginning to look at the behaviour and actions of the Director of Public Works from a different angle.

Nineteen

◇

ALADE MOSES lost the election petition case, and as expected the Opposition made much of his losing it. Under a front-page editorial 'Judgement of the Just' the editor of the *Sentinel* wrote: 'All lovers of truth and of cleanliness in public life will hail the judgement of the Supreme Court which yesterday declared null and void the election of the Minister of Works the Honourable Alade Moses in the Newtown North Constituency. We of this paper have at no time entertained any doubt in our mind about the outcome of the case. We do not need to hold university degrees in constitutional law or be members of the learned profession to know that anyone like Alade Moses who entered the Legislative House through the window of machinations of a bigoted tribal union instead of going through the front door of electoral regulations will be chucked out of the sacred House.

'We of this paper have been justified in our unshaken belief in the unlimited capacity of our judiciary to absorb the stresses and strains to which this unholy gang of rascals who have now forced themselves upon the nation have subjected the judges and the magistrates. In the dark days of every nation when rogues and dictators seize the reins of government it has always been the impartiality, fearlessness, and incorruptibility of the custodians of justice that have always stood between man and doom. We are proud to record here to the eternal glory of the judiciary of this land that in spite of threats and intimidation, most times subtle and concealed but sometimes open, they have carried out their sacred duty of administering justice, just justice, in the highest tradition of their most sacred calling.

'It is a matter for shame and much regret that the central figure in this case is one of the most brilliant intellectuals that this young nation has produced. A man whose proven integrity was known once to match his great intellect. Once, that was. For unfortunately Alade Moses Esq., Bachelor of Arts of the University of London, Holder of the Diploma in Education of the same University, one time the hard hitting and honest Treasurer of the Afromacolese Students Union of Great Britain and Ireland, has collapsed like a pack of cards before the evil and corrupting influence of the gang of crooks who are his fellow travellers. It is most sad and unfortunate that this once beloved and respected leader of thought has descended to the low level of appearing at the wedding feast of the lawmaking institution of the nation without an invitation card. And that is why we must not be sorry for him when yesterday he suffered the fate of his predecessor of bible fame:

> Friend, how camest thou in hither
> not having a wedding garment? . . .
> Bind him hand and foot, and take
> him away, and cast him into outer
> darkness . . .

'One final word for Alade Moses to note. There is one and only one course of action for a gentleman of honour to take in the present situation. Resign. Resign from the Cabinet; resign from the lawmaking assembly of the nation. Apologize to the electorate that you have wronged. Tell them that you have left undone those things which you ought to have done, and that you have done those things which you ought not to have done. Then put yourself forward in competition with other sons of Newtown for the seat for Newtown but this time via the only recognized door of the electoral regulations. There is redemption for the sinner that truly repents and turns back from his wrong doing. But we know that your colleagues, the dishonourable pack of Honourable members of the House, will advise you otherwise. Listen to them and a fate worse than the Supreme Court judgement awaits you. We have spoken.'

In the middle of the morning on the day the leader appeared in the *Sentinel*, Alade Moses called on the Prime Minister.

'Come right in, Minister. Come right in,' the Prime Minister said in a tired voice.

'I'm so sorry to bother you at this time, sir,' Moses said, as he closed the door behind him.

'You are welcome at all times, Minister,' the Prime Minister cut short the apologies.

'I hope you are very much better, sir,' Moses said as he sat in the chair opposite the Prime Minister at the other side of the desk. Moses noticed that this was a new desk made in the new furniture factory in Moyamba. It was of local timber and was very beautifully finished. He thought that the critics of Government's partnership arrangement with the Jordarmenian concern that supplied the technical management of the furniture factory ought to see this beautiful desk and how it did the study of the Premier's Lodge proud.

'Better, d'you say? I'm perfect,' the Prime Minister exclaimed.

'But you are under Doctor's orders to have absolute —'

'Doctor's orders! The fellow's mad. Thinks he can play

that game with me. You see it's all right when we doctors have laymen as our patients – as we do most of the time. We can deceive the layman patient into believing that he's got some disease and that only we can cure him. First we call it a long Latin name. That is the first thing that beats the patient. Then we write a prescription in a language that is compounded of Latin and algebra. Then —' here the medico–politician suddenly stopped. He looked through his visitor as if he were not there. To the embarrassment of Moses, the Prime Minister began to hold a dialogue with what in effect was a second guest invisible to Moses. The language was completely incomprehensible to Moses. Embarrassment turned to fright. For it had been freely said in Cabinet and party circles that the Prime Minister had gone queer upstairs. Here was Moses witnessing the embarrassing truth in the Prime Minister's own study. 'Ah, my illness, yes my illness,' the Prime Minister said in a come-back-to-earth voice, to Moses' relief. 'I myself was the first to realize that what was wrong with me was unknown to European medicine.'

'Yes, sir?' Moses said, his face showing polite curiosity.

'Quite. That was why I wouldn't hear for a moment Franco-John's suggestion of my being flown to Geneva to a specialist neurologist. Waste of Government funds. Waste of time. It's now gone. I'm perfectly all right. Thanks to your Chief Odole. Lucky you have such a useful relation, Minister.'

'Yes, sir,' Moses said mechanically, feeling the juju belt Chief Odole gave him five months before. So the Prime Minister, a Member of the Royal College of Surgeons of Great Britain, had gone the juju way when he fell ill: he recalled the impressive list of the clients of the juju Malaam that Chief Odole gave him the day he gave him the belt.

Moses told the Prime Minister that he had come in to tender his resignation from the Cabinet and from the House.

He brought out the four sheets of type-written matter, the original and a copy of the letter of resignation.

'The usual sentiments,' the Prime Minister said as he glanced through the papers. 'Circumstances beyond control, et cetera et cetera et cetera. Pleasure and honour serving under you and being given the opportunity of participating in the formulation of policy and the execution of that policy as it pertained to the administration of the Ministry of Works —'

The Prime Minister got up and paced his study. Then he said, 'I had anticipated your move, Minister. I knew exactly what you were going to do. Let me say at the outset that you truly have a problem on your hands. I am so sorry that all these troubles have piled up on your head. Most unfair. Most unfair.'

'Thank you sir.'

'It was truly a bad mistake your people made not to have observed the electoral regulations. I understand that you would have won hands down and that it was absolutely unnecessary to have ignored the provisions of the regulations.'

'I agree with you sir. Absolutely unnecessary to have prevented Dauda's man from filing his own nomination papers. Still —'

'I've had a word with Franco about it. As things were the Chief Justice couldn't have done anything. Absolutely nothing . . . There really was no need appealing to the Supreme Court. in the first instance, Minister. We shall now leave the courts out of it. Dauda and his boys may think they have beaten us. But have they?'

'It does appear so, at least this time, sir.'

'It does appear so. But is it really so, Minister?'

Alade Moses looked at the Prime Minister questioningly. The P.M. had now resumed his seat.

'I accept your letter of resignation from both the Cabinet

and the House, with the usual expressions of regret and gratitude for your most invaluable services to the nation and your unflinching loyalty to and support for me personally et cetera et cetera et cetera.'

One of the four telephones rang. The Prime Minister ignored it. However he stopped talking while the ringing lasted. Then he continued: 'Resigning from the Cabinet and from the House is in the best tradition of parliamentary behaviour. This will satisfy your personal sense of honour – which I know is high.'

'Thank you sir,' Moses muttered.

'It will also satisfy those who watch our activities from abroad. Our British and American friends. Above all it will satisfy our critics, Dauda and his gang. At least for some time. That is till you are back in the Cabinet as soon as His Excellency signs the Special Warrant tomorrow.'

'I do not understand sir,' Moses said, looking into the face of the older man.

'You see under Section Twenty Four Subsection Three of the Constitution the Prime Minister has power to appoint three Special Members of the House of Assembly. Such members must be persons who in addition to satisfying the requirements of being electors as set out in Sections Fifty-Three to Sixty-One must appear to possess special attributes which appear to the Prime Minister will enhance the business of the House. You Alad. Moses appear to me to possess such attributes and I have decided and directed that you be appointed a Special Member of the House.'

'But sir —'

'Yes?'

'It is the wisdom of it I'm wondering about. What people will say.'

'The wisdom of it – that's the whole point. What's the wisdom in disqualifying from further service to the nation a Minister of State of proven ability and proven integrity, one that has laid the foundations for the superstructure of our ambitious programme in road, waterworks, and building construction? Why must we now begin to look round for another fellow with ability in a pool of human resources that is very scanty indeed? Damn it all, man. I am bent on having the best team and keeping it, regardless of Dauda and his crowd.' The Prime Minister spoke with authority and conviction. Moses saw that.

'You will give me time to think about it, sir.'

'Think about it by all means. But you have already accepted the offer, my dear chap. The Solicitor General has prepared the warrants for H.E.'s signature. The first warrant for your appointment as a Special Member. The second as a Minister of State. And by the way I hear your people have honoured you with a chieftaincy title, eh?'

'Sir?' Moses appeared not to understand.

'I think Franco organized it – with your kinsman Chief Odole. If they haven't told you yet they must be thinking of springing a surprise on you. A chieftaincy title will buttress your position as Minister of State.'

Twenty

———————◇———————

ALADE MOSES had returned from the interview with the Prime Minister more confused than he was before he went in. He had known that he had to resign before the leader that came out in the *Sentinel*. He had known that the Prime Minister would express his disappointment at the way the election petition case had gone, his sincere appreciation for his services, and his profound regret for his having to leave the Government in the circumstances that were beyond the control of either of them. But he had thought that the Prime Minister would accept his resignation after these usual expressions of sentiments. Yes, that was what he had thought would happen.

What would he do for a living after? He had also given thought to this before he went to see the Prime Minister. He was not keen on going back to Newtown Grammar School. Geo Abyssinia was already well entrenched there and was getting on fine with the Newtown Improvement Union, which was synonymous with the authorities of the school, in spite of the fact that he was devoting more time to his contract business than to the affairs of the school. Moses was sure that he would be as unwelcome in the school as he was reluctant to go back to it. He had thought that the Prime Minister would offer him the chairmanship of a new

Corporation, the recently found method of compensating with juicy jobs important party supporters after they had been rejected at the polls. Franco-John was said to have submitted to the Prime Minister the day the election petition case was decided proposals for a new Housing Corporation which would both keep Moses employed and at the same time fix some money at regular intervals for the party funds. Moses was sorry he was already mixed up in a number of things which brought a question mark to his integrity. But he was determined that he would not add this to the existing tally of shame. No, he would refuse to be chairman of a new corporation. That was his determination. But now look at the Prime Minister's solution! Retaining his seat in the House and in the Cabinet by way of Section Twenty-Four, Subsection Three! He gave serious thought to the complications and the implications. He was sure it would lead to no good. His reputation was already sinking. His enemies would again get hold of this and hound him out of the House. Indeed, his political adversaries apart, he did not share the Prime Minister's happiness at the fact that he would be arriving in the House this time not through the entrance door but via the window. He shuddered at what the opposition paper would say about this. Indeed it did not require his critics to remind him that in the good old days the Afromacolese society had a name for those who preferred to enter a house through the window to doing so through the door. Rogues!

But the chieftaincy idea appealed to him. He had since the beginning of his parliamentary career been fascinated by the discovery that there was blue blood in his veins, the discovery that had been announced by Gorgeous Gregory when he was reading the 'Illuminated Address' that was presented to him at the reception the Newtown Improvement Union gave him on his appointment as a Minister of State eleven and a half months before.

Blue blood in his veins! His father who died when he was still an infant was known to be an ordinary drummer. His mother did not talk much about him or about his family. Every indication was that there wasn't much good to talk about anyway. He recalled that when he was a pupil teacher preparing by correspondence course for his London Matriculation he had written love letters to Lola, then a young Newtown girl on holidays from the teacher-training college in Moyamba. Her mother who was a leading member of the church community had gone to report him to the vicar who was also the manager of the school. Did the pupil teacher not know that her daughter came from a warrior family in the land and that she was to be protected against the advances of nobodies like Alade Moses? When the time came for the girl to have a husband, the mother had said haughtily, they in her family knew where not to look for one. He recalled how Lola was eventually sent overseas for further education, and how she had come back with qualifications that the Ministry of Education officials said were worthless. Eventually, he recalled, she had been given a secretary's post in that very Ministry. In spite of his own exalted position, Moses still smarted under the slight meted out to him by Lola's people years back. The mother was now an old woman, but still a leader in the church community. She was illiterate. But even an illiterate old woman knew that Ministers of State were important personalities, more important than the oba in the community – the oba they had known in days gone by as second in importance only to the gods. All the community now knew that he was as well descended as any in the land. That old woman would hear this. Her daughter would hear it. They would both regret as they were already regretting, he was sure, their having discouraged him from proceeding with the courtship nine years before.

He decided to fight the election. He was sure he would

win. He was convinced that he was still a favourite with his people, the opposition and their attacks on him in their press notwithstanding. He would also be installed a chief. His kinsman Chief Odole would steer him through the tiring ceremony – the visit to shrine after shrine and the rites to be performed at each shrine. From then onwards he would be addressed Chief Alade Moses, B.A., Dip.Ed., the Honourable Minister of Works. Chief The Honourable Minister! He would have arrived completely then. He wondered for a moment how the Afromacolese Students Union of Great Britain and Ireland would take it. Then he wondered why he should bother about how they took it. As the Minister of Home Affairs had observed at a Cabinet meeting which discussed a letter which the Union wrote to Alade Moses criticizing his political and unpatriotic activities, no one should take the boys seriously. 'They are youths at the dangerous age when they think they are next to God Almighty in knowledge,' that was the Minister's description of the students in Britain. 'It's only after they come back home and face the realities of life and of administration that they will discover that their education is just beginning.'

Moses recalled that Franco-John held a different view. 'These boys are at a dangerous age all right. And they are dangerous through and through. I think we must be careful about them.'

Local Government: 'What d'you think we should do, then?'

Home Affairs: 'Minister of Works to sue the Secretary and the President, and the entire Union members for libel.' It was difficult to tell whether he was serious or merely pulling Moses' leg.

Alade Moses: 'No, thank you. I've done enough suing for libel to last me for the rest of my political career.'

Franco-John, frowning at the laughter raised by the observation of Alade Moses: 'This is no laughing matter at all. Those boys in London are dangerous. About time someone called a halt to their subversive activities.'

Local Government: 'Communists. The whole lot of them. Communists and fellow-travellers.'

Franco-John: 'We must not all sit here complacently till they come to kick us all out in a revolution. I've advised the Minister of Education to withdraw the scholarships of those of them that are Government scholars.' (One long suck at the current cigarette before crushing the remains in the ash-tray.)

Home Affairs: 'But then they would be stranded.'

Prime Minister (noting the alarm of the Minister of Home Affairs): 'I think we are taking this matter too seriously. Much too seriously. The letter to the Minister of Works is no more than an exhibition of youthful exuberance. It is present in all university students throughout the world. A sign of healthy growth in the youth of the nation, that's what it is. I think we should now go on to the more pressing items on our heavy agenda.'

All that had happened seven weeks before. Since then he had lost his seat in the House and his post in the Cabinet. He would now fight the election and get into the House in a way that even the prudish, look-at-us-we-are-holy boys in London would not be able to assail.

One afternoon nine days later Gorgeous Gregory nearly drove him mad when he told him that he would require a sum of £12,000 to fight the by-election. Moses reported the matter to Franco-John and took the opportunity to tell the older politician of his intention to do away with Gregory's services in the by-election campaign. He reminded Franco-John of the bitter fact that it was Gorgeous Gregory that had bungled the original election. Gorgeous Gregory and his kinsman Chief Odole. See the price he had now been called upon to pay for their senseless folly.

'I don't think you need as much as £12,000,' Franco-John observed, appearing to be doing some mental arithmetic. The meeting was in the lounge of his ministerial quarters. 'No, I don't think you need that much —'

'£12,000! Why, I've decided I shan't bribe anyone in this campaign. Not a penny. I'm determined about that.' He stamped his foot to give force to his determination.

'I should guess you will get in comfortably on £6,000, Alade – have a cigarette.' He lit himself a new one from the smouldering stub of its predecessor.

'£6,000!' Moses exclaimed, lighting his own cigarette.

'Oh £5,000, £6,000. Something in that neighbourhood, you know.'

'But I've just told you I shan't bribe anyone. I refuse to. I'm absolutely decided on that.' He smoked furiously.

'But you don't have to bribe anyone, man. You see there are certain election expenses which you just have to run. You cannot escape them. Take my case as an example. Mine is a most comfortable seat – the result of keeping excellent relations with the party leaders in my constituency.'

'Yes'?

'Here in Victoria I have three clerks and in Moyamba two. These are full time employees. Salary is – er – £45 a month. That's £540 a year. With rents and stationery that's something like £900 a year.' (Changing of cigarettes ceremony comparable in solemnity with changing of guards.)

'Really?' Moses looked at him inquiringly.

'Really. Six months to the election I employ eight field officers. Local boys, Standard VI passed. Salary at £6 a month for six months – that's er —'

'£288.'

'Nearly £300. Add to that the cost of six Raleigh bicycles. Sulaiman let me have them cheap at £25 each. That's £25 in six places. £150. This together with £300 makes £450. We pick up the existing – er – £900. We are now £1,350.'

'Most interesting. Most interesting,' Moses muttered.

'Very interesting indeed. Then two months to D-day you purchase two jeeps.'

'But the Party sends each candidate one, doesn't it?'

'Yes, one jeep. But the Opposition sent six jeeps to my constituency last time. You know it is a key constituency, because of me. I don't even remember the cost of each of the two jeeps I bought. But I assure you I paid every penny of it to Joe Arden despite that libellous publication of Dauda in his yellow sheet.'

'I see,' Alade Moses said distantly, apparently trying to figure the whole thing out.

'Then the money allocation to the wards and quarters, to the various clubs and societies, through the village and ward heads, and the presidents and secretaries of the clubs. Allocation usually varies from £5 to £50, depending on the size and status of the body concerned. The money is not a bribe at all, contrary to the allegation of arm-chair critics who are very much removed from reality, and too conceited and prejudiced to really find out what's going on.'

'I see?' again Moses said inquiringly.

'It's money for feasting the people. You see either once a week or once a fortnight these people meet, in the house of the village or ward head, or in the parlour of the president, to deliberate upon the affairs of their organization. At these meetings they take turns to feast themselves, consuming keg after keg of palm wine – My God, how those people drink!' he said as he performed the inevitable ceremony of changing cigarettes.

'I thought it's beer people drink these days.'

'Yes, you are right. Palm wine and beer nowadays. Drinks and food the quantity and quality of which they normally would not have in their own homes for the rest of the week.' After a brief pause, Franco-John continued. 'If you want people to vote for you, they first have to accept you as a member of their ward or of their club. Your payment of £20 or so is for your representative to organize on your behalf the feasting of the club or society for one Sunday – their acceptance of you as one of them. You see what I mean?'

'Most revealing,' Moses commented thoughtfully.

'And from this time to election day both your house and the houses of some dozen of your supporters become the meeting places for your agents. Here they meet in the morning to plan the day's campaign. And here they meet at night to receive and review the reports of the day's activities. Breakfast in the morning, supper at night; each lubricated with palm wine and beer – and gin and whisky for the sophisticated. And nearly everybody is sophisticated these days, my dear chap. All at your expense. All perfectly legitimate expenses.'

Later that night Alade Moses gave serious thought to his position. He pondered the legitimate expenses that Franco-John ran in a safe constituency. Franco-John had not included the payments to lorry and taxi drivers for free transportation of voters on election day – and Moses knew this was the practice. If Franco-John spent all this in a safe constituency, what would he spend – legitimately spend – in a constituency that Dauda had contaminated with evil and foul propaganda against him? He remembered Gorgeous Gregory and wondered if his figure of £12,000 was as ridiculous as he had thought. In spite of the cooling effect of the October storm, he rolled from side to side on his bed, the victim of his doubts and his ambition.

Twenty One

---◇---

SEVENTEEN days before the by-election Government approved the appointment of Alade Moses as the Asiwaju, a chieftaincy which meant Prime Minister of Newtown. Government approval was required because it was a major chieftaincy: nothing short of a major chieftaincy would rebuild the damaged image of the ex-Minister.

The installation ceremony was a joint affair of the new chief, the Newtown Improvement Union and the Freedom for All Party. For the third time in thirty-one months Moses was again the centre of a very colourful and loud ceremony except that this time the quality of the attendance had gone up by the presence of not three but eleven Ministers of State headed by the Prime Minister himself. Also 'gracing the occasion' with their presence, as the pro-Government paper described it the following day, were eight foreign ambassadors and High Commissioners from Commonwealth countries.

'Freeman, Freeman, why aren't you filming them now?' the anguished voice of the Film Director of the Voice of Afromacoland boomed over the loudspeaker, in spite of the terrific noise of drumming, bugling, singing, shouting, and chattering all going on at one and the same time.

'But the European, sir. He —' the voice of the official

cameraman at the ceremony also boomed over the loud-speaker.

'Which European, you stupid man?' the Director queried.

'That one sir, the one with the camera sir,' the cameraman indicated the Jordarmenian Ambassador at that moment very busy with his cine-camera focused on a group of dancing women gorgeously dressed in their 'aso-ebi' swaying their waists appealingly to the tune of the 'Shekere' orchestra. 'He told us to hold on for him to take just one or two shots, sir.'

'Come on, foolish man. I suppose it's after the women have gone to sit down before you begin to run about. And – good Lord!' It was at this stage that the film boss realized that his not-so-friendly dialogue with his subordinate was being magnified through the mysteries of electronics and was to his embarrassment and confusion providing much welcome side entertainment for the huge crowd.

'What spectacle, what splendour!' the Jordarmenian Ambassador said excitedly as he adjusted the cine slung across his shoulder, beaming at the wife of the American Ambassador next to whom he was sitting.

'Sure, gorgeous,' she exclaimed like a high-school girl on a picnic.

'What a glimpse of a most ancient tradition, outcrop of a most ancient culture, a vanished civilization – er-er-er-tsho, tshoo, tshoo – pardon me,' the diplomat collapsed in a fit of sneezing.

While all this was going on among the distinguished guests and the multitude of not-so-distinguished Newtown citizens outside, the eyes of the new chief were just adjusting themselves to the very poor illumination in the fifth and last of the shrines at which he had performed different obligatory rites. It was more correct to say that he had had performed for him different rites which he ought to have performed by himself.

The deity to be worshipped here was represented by a clay pot, about the size and shape women used for boiling yams preparatory to pounding for the evening meal of 'iyon' with soup. Even in the partial darkness he saw the difference. This sacred pot did not have a soot-covered body. It had been rubbed brownish red with some white symbols chalked on. While the chief priest, who with his kinsman and patron Chief Odole had been piloting him from shrine to shrine, began to recite some incantations and philosophy in poetic language his mind went back to a short period in his unedifying childhood when he and his mother lived with his maternal grandmother in her village. Why they lived there he did not remember. But he remembered that in Granny's room in the mud-walled compound house in the village there were two pots. One was an ordinary pot in which drinking water was stored. The other was Granny's deity, in colouring and shape remarkably similar to the one before which he was now worshipping.

The squawking of the white cock with which the priest touched his forehead three times brought him back from his dive into the innocent days of his childhood to the reality of his being the centre of the heathen rite now going on: he, Alade Moses, Bachelor of Arts of the University of London, holder of the Diploma in Education from the same University, he Alade Moses with all this evidence of civilization and knowledge, now prostrating before idols. Yes, he had prostrated before two of the four which they had visited before this one. He had had to kneel and touch the ground with his forehead at the first of the shrines. And – good Lord – he shrank with fright and horror as the priest wrung the neck of the squawking cock and directed the spurt of blood from the headless trunk on to the deity, all the time reciting incantations. He became dizzy and sick when he saw the priest dip one finger in the blood and dab his forehead with the horrible mess. Was this he – Alade, baptized into the Christian Church and given the Jewish name of Moses as was the custom of the church in those days? Was this he who recited the Ten Commandments before the vicar of the local church when he examined the candidates, seventeen boys and eleven girls, before the baptism? He saw then the picture of the vicar as he asked him to recite the First Commandment. And he remembered how he did it, parrot-wise:

'Thou shalt have no other gods before me.'

'Second Commandment?'

'Thou shalt not make unto thee any graven image or any likeness of anything that is in heaven above, or that is in the earth beneath, or that is in the water under the earth.

'Thou shalt not bow down thyself to them nor serve them: for I the Lord thy God am a jealous God, visiting the iniquities of the fathers upon the children, unto the third and fourth generation of them that hate me.

'And showing mercy unto thousands of them that love me, and keep my commandments' (and keep my command-ments . . . and keep my commandments . . . and keep . . . and keep . . .) Alade Moses had been overcome by the stench and the heat.

A long while after there was a sudden increase in the intensity of the drumming and the shouting in the crowd. There was some rushing of people from the direction of the palace, and a stirring among the distinguished guests in the V.I.P. stand.

'I think something is about to happen now,' the wife of the British High Commissioner said excitedly. She battled to keep her broad-brimmed hat on her head as she strained her neck.

'Yes, the new chief will come out of the shrines any time now,' Franco-John who sat next to her enlightened her.

'How interesting! How very interesting!'

'Yes, very interesting indeed,' Franco-John confirmed.

'But tell me. Chief, has he now received from the ancestors the mystic power Charles talks of in his book?' the diminutive Englishwoman asked, quite excited.

'Charles?' Franco-John looked blank. He'd never heard the name before. Reading of any sort was not one of his vices.

'Professor Charles! *Chieftaincy Institutions and Chieftaincy Rites in an African Tribe*. You must read it, Chief. It is a must,' she smiled, exhibiting an ugly set of teeth even by English standards.

'I'd love to,' he lied.

'Well, let me lend you my copy. But you must promise to return it. You promise?'

'Yes,' he said, irritated by this discussion of a subject in which he was not the least interested.

The excitement and shouting in the crowd had increased, More of the people who obviously had been taking part in the rites in the shrines had come out. The combined team of Government and Native Authority police had the greatest job keeping the excited crowd from breaking through into the opening in front and to the right of the V.I.P. stand.

A sudden burst of dane-gun shots from the direction of the shrines rocked the whole place and thoroughly frightened the V.I.P. guests who did not immediately understand what it was about.

'Nothing to worry about,' Franco-John smiled at the wife of the British High Commissioner.

'Oh, Chief, I *was* frightened,' she said breathlessly, the colour returning to her face. 'Ah, here he comes. George, over there.'

'Yes, here he comes,' her husband Sir George Hardcastle repeated after her.

'Isn't he gorgeous! Isn't he *beautiful*! Oh George, just *look* at that.'

'Yes, my dear,' the British High Commissioner said into his whiskers. He was doing his best to conceal his contempt for his Jordarmenian colleague who had thrown all diplomatic dignity to the wind and was at that moment fighting with the 'Voice of Afromacoland' cameraman for a position of vantage from which to take shots of the procession now coming towards the V.I.P. stand.

As they all stood while the new chief was being escorted to his seat at the V.I.P. stand, Franco-John wondered how much of the excitement shown by Lady Margaret Hardcastle was genuine and how much was traditional British hypocrisy. He himself did not see anything beautiful or gorgeous in the simple white 'dansiki' and trousers worn by Alade Moses. Tradition did not permit of expensive clothes being worn on the day of installation; this was reserved for the Iwuye ceremony when the new chief could and would wear very rich sanyon robes with voluminous sleeves. Then in addition to the chieftaincy beads which he now wore he would wear a long gold chain round his neck. Surely all these expatriates who were excited over the whole ceremony had seen Alade Moses in a more gorgeous setting before!

'George, do you know something?' Margaret Hardcastle said to her husband.

'Yes, dear?' George Hardcastle inclined his head towards her. Just a little. More than that would detract from the dignity that surrounded the diplomatic status. It did not matter that one was talking to one's wife.

'Look at his face,' she said, pointing her fan in the direction of the new chief.

'Yes,' George Hardcastle did. He did not immediately see what his wife wanted him to see in the face of Alade Moses. Was is the red smudge of blood and the black of some powder that she wanted attention focused on?

'Don't you see that this face bears remarkable resemblance to the Shongay head at the Museum in Victoria?'

'Yes, dear. Now you say it, I believe you are right,' George Hardcastle confirmed.

'The perfect Shongay forehead. Isn't that wonderful? But George?'

'Yes, dear?'

'He's looking *strange*. He's tired!'

Alade Moses was looking strange. He was tired. The physical exertion of going from shrine to shrine; the mental strain of drinking potions and partaking of concoctions the composition of which he did not know, the taste of which he did not like, the thought of which now sickened him; all these things were necessary, big Uncle Chief Odole had warned him. Every one of them had a role to play in the warding off of the evil spirits associated with the chieftaincy. The combined weight of all this was now telling on him.

Gorgeous Gregory, Master of Ceremony, started the speech-making, the part of the ceremony in which the Ministers and other politicians could join in to the political advantage of the new chief. 'My Lord Bishop, Spiritual Fathers in the Lord, Chief Imam, Honourable Ministers of State, Chiefs, Ladies and Gentlemen, this is a red letter day in the annals of our beloved city Newtown.' Again Moses recollected that was the third time in thirty-one months that Gorgeous Gregory had designated a day red. He also recollected that he, Moses, had in each case been the principal character in the ceremony, the hero that had made each red letter day a deeper hue than the one immediately preceding it. His tired mind dived into the past and pondered the doings on those other two occasions. The day the Newtown Improvement Union had received him on his return from Britain and his appointment as the Principal of the Grammar School, and the other one when the same Union had honoured him as the first Newtown man to be appointed a Minister of State. That was exactly twelve months before.

Chief Odole spoke. The President of the Improvement Union spoke. The new chief dozed off for minutes at a time. For how long he had been slumbering in his exposed, exalted position he could not tell when he eventually yawned himself awake, to the amusement of his V.I.P. colleagues. It was the Prime Minister now addressing the gathering. How long he had been speaking Moses could not tell. 'We are all here today not just because he belongs to our great Party but because he is a great man with whom we are proud to associate . . . We are proud of the activities and achievements of your most progressive Improvement Union that has been the pace setter for other tribal unions . . . Above all we are glad that you have by conferring this chieftaincy on your greatest son helped him, you have helped us, you have helped this nation, to rediscover this great man, this prophet that has been going in and coming out among you in this progressive town without your recognizing his worth, his noble ancestry . . .

'A great English scholar once observed that when we see genius come out of what looks like the gutter we should know that it did not begin there. If we take the trouble to dig beneath the surface we will discover that like Shakespeare the son of a wood-pedlar, Napoleon the son of a farmer, and Luther the son of a peasant, the genius from the gutter most probably descended from a line of kings and prophets. That observation was made about one of the greatest figures of history, Abraham Lincoln. It may well be applied here and now to your own son Alade Moses, who we join you to honour today. Today we congratulate you on publicly recognizing the great line of chiefs and sages from which this your great son descended. We congratulate you on re-discovering the great potentiality in Chief the Honourable Alade Moses, the – er – Aṣiwaju of Newtown. We now ask you, people of Newtown, to help us to help you by voting, all of you, for your new chief on Thursday at the by-election. Help us build up this great son and chief of Newtown, this great nationalist and hard-hitting fighter in the relentless struggle against the imperialist in the worthy cause of freedom for all, this great man, this great statesman, and, by this vote of you the good people of this great town, this future Prime Minister of our great country Afromacoland.'

Twenty-two

CHIEF the Honourable Alade Moses, M.P., B.A. (Hons.),
Dip.Ed., Minister of Works, the Aṣiwaju of Newtown. This
was now his full title. It looked impressive both on the
green-edged official card and the fine quality notepaper
which Gorgeous Gregory had organized for him immediately after his installation as a chief of Newtown.

His latest attempt at bringing back his erring feet to the
path of political rectitude had failed due to circumstances
over which he had little control; he had not been able to
carry out his resolution to reject the offer of the Prime
Minister to make him a Special Member of the House in
which capacity he would continue as a Minister of State.
The Jordarmenian firm of contractors had introduced what
was described as a pilot housing scheme for Ministers of
State and Parliamentary Secretaries. Under this scheme a
house was designed and built for each Minister or Parliamentary Secretary on a plot of land owned by him. The firm
financed the cost of the house in the first instance. The
beneficiary then paid back the cost together with interest at
the relatively low rate of $3\frac{1}{2}\%$ over a period of five years,
repayment commencing from the end of the month in which
the house was completed. As it happened the big extra-
modern two-storey building erected for Moses under this

scheme was completed in the same month that the election petition case was decided against him. As he had no other source of income from which to meet the monthly repayments, he agreed with his colleagues and Gloria that it would be criminal folly not to accept the Prime Minister's offer.

The position therefore was that even though he had ceased to be Member of Parliament for the Newtown North Constituency, his membership of the House and tenure of office as a Minister of State continued uninterrupted. And his £250 a month salary and numerous allowances continued to be paid to him. He, however, remained the Government Party candidate for the by-election.

The electioneering was hotting up on both sides. Moses had been advised, indeed ordered by the party hierarchy, to leave the electioneering to those who knew how to do it. However he managed to get in return a promise that hooliganism and thuggery would be kept to a minimum and that nothing would be done this time that would land him in another petition case.

Nine days before the by-election Dauda attacked him and Government in a front page article in the *Sentinel*. The article alleged that not only was the Government financing the by-election expenses in Newtown but there was incontrovertible evidence to show that it had financed the expenses of the chieftaincy installation ceremony at Newtown. It dwelt at length on the punishment that awaited those responsible for this gross waste of the taxpayers' money on the senseless, selfish aggrandisement of a young man who had since fallen from grace to grass. It then alleged something else that shocked and frightened Moses, namely that Moses and his supporters were administering oaths secretly to people to force them to vote for him.

He was not much worried about the allegation of Govern-

ment funds being used on his behalf. He knew that techni-
cally this was not true. What was true was that the proceeds
from the ten per cent rake-offs from contracts were being
used for this purpose. Franco-John had persuaded him that
this was precisely how elections were run in the so-called
civilized countries. He did not waste his conscience over
this part of the article. But he was worried about the oath-
taking allegation. He called Gorgeous Gregory and told him
to read the article.

'I think the Attorney General should see this, Minister,'
Gregory said, having read the article half way. 'I'd phone
now —'

'Gorgeous, let us keep the Attorney General out of this,'
Moses hissed.

'But Minister, our good name has again been libelled.'

'Look, forget about the first part of the article. Fact is
I'm fed up. The word libel sickens me. No more libel cases
for me, you hear? It's the second bit of the article
I'm worried about. The oath-taking. What's all this
about?'

'The oath-taking?' Gorgeous Gregory whistled in
surprise. He glanced through the rest of the article. Then
he said: 'Well, to speak the truth I think Chief is doing
that.'

'Chief Odole is running the oath-taking racket! It is true
then?' Moses looked perplexed.

Gorgeous Gregory looked into his glass guiltily.

After a long pause during which Alade Moses fidgeted
with the juju ring on the second left finger he said slowly:
'Gorgeous Gregory, I'm really worried about the things you
do. I mean you and Chief Odole. You know very well that
oath-taking and the administration of oaths is against the
electoral regulations. You know all this trouble of a by-
election would not have arisen if you people had observed
the electoral regulations in the first instance. I am still to

understand why you people will continue to keep me ignorant of actions you purport to be taking on my behalf.'

'But Minister, there's —'

'Look, man, there's one thing I want to know. Just who is the candidate for this by-election? You, Gorgeous Gregory, or me? Or Chief Odole? Just answer me that question.'

Long after Gorgeous Gregory had gone, Moses sat in his chair in the lounge thoroughly displeased with himself. Again the thought came to him for the umpteenth time that he must take a stand somewhere. There must be a limit to the dishonourable acts that he would allow his name to be associated with. But again for the umpteenth time the realization came to him that his action was now ill-timed and belated. And again he remembered the decision at the party meeting that he must leave the electioneering to be done by the people who knew best how to do it – the Gregorys and the Chief Odoles and the Franco-Johns. So much was at stake that the party could not afford to lose the by-election. Whatever he felt at that time he had not protested. Now that D-day was only nine days away his action in protesting against the criminal and immoral methods being adopted by his agents looked like hypocrisy. It was hypocrisy.

He was sorry about his eruption against Gregory. While he'd been wanting to kick the man out for some time he thought he'd chosen the wrong time. And he really had to be careful about the chap. He knew far too much of his personal secrets and of state secrets that it was most unwise to anger him now. The rogue! Moses was aware of the man's dishonesty, how he had made so much money in various deals. He knew how much time he spent in the houses of Abyssinia and of the Jordarmenian Ambassador. He knew that his own name must have been involved in matters about which he knew nothing but which had brought

Gorgeous Gregory and the Newtown Improvement Union monetary benefits.

Gorgeous Gregory hurried to Newtown and reported the strange behaviour of the candidate to Chief Odole and two other leaders of the local branch of the Party. They came to the conclusion that the things that Alade Moses had gone through in the immediately preceding weeks were enough to affect the mind of anyone – the threat to the ministerial post, and the chieftaincy installation ceremony. He was to be pitied rather than condemned. The campaign was to go on as planned. What the candidate's feelings and wishes were must not be allowed to interfere with the programme of the Party.

They reviewed the situation as regarded the oath-taking ceremony, in view of the unfortunate publication in the *Sentinel*. Gorgeous Gregory said that Franco-John had always alleged that they had fifth columnists in their rank in Newtown. Otherwise how did the thing get into the *Sentinel*?

'Through the Police of course. The whole lot of them are in the pay of Dauda and his gang,' the local Party treasurer said bitterly.

'But we saw the Police Chief, didn't we?' Gorgeous Gregory asked.

'How can you ask such a question, as if you didn't know the details?' the Treasurer said, appearing resentful of a suggestion that money approved for passing on to this important functionary of Government might not have reached its destination, a thing that would be calling his integrity into question. 'And it wasn't only the Commissioner that we saw. We saw both the Deputy and the Assistant Deputy.'

'I hear Dauda and his gang saw them too,' Chief Odole observed seriously. 'But I'm sure they couldn't find anything near the amount we gave. I'm sure of that,' the old man said, confirming his belief in what he said by spitting and stamping his bare left foot on the bare concrete floor of his ill-ventilated sitting-room.

Gorgeous Gregory told his companions that they could not be too sure of that. He was in possession of information of a very secret nature that the Opposition had received a very large sum of money from a foreign government through trade union channels. The money was for trade union organization but Dauda's Opposition Party were using it to subvert the Government and to fight elections. As for the police, Gorgeous Gregory said that he had no doubt in his mind that the other side had given them money. In fact he had agreed with the police chief that whatever money the Opposition offered him he should accept and pretend to be working for them. Why shouldn't he take money from both sides? Was it not God that had placed him in this position which was about the best money-making one in the Government service? What was important was that the police boss should keep his word with the Government Party. And he was sure he would, for the friendship between him and the police boss went beyond party politics. He just could not deceive him. They all agreed to accept Gorgeous Gregory's views on the matter. The publication in the paper being due to the police was not as strange as it first appeared. After all, they had all heard what happened at the Owari Shrine.

Later that night Gorgeous Gregory met the Commissioner of Police in the three-roomed flat of Lola his girl friend. While Lola went about some typing which she said Derek McDonald had given her, the police boss and Gregory talked the serious matter over in her bedroom.

Twenty-three

◇

The boisterous laughing in the ground floor lounge of the V.I.P. rest house in Moyamba subsided for a moment as the knocking on the door was repeated.

'Who's there?' the Minister of Local Government demanded, recharging his glass of stout.

'It's me, sir. I want the Minister of Education.'

'Obviously another female for you, Minister,' Titus Badejo said in a whisper. He shook his head ominously: Education was going to the door to intercept his fair caller and decide whether she could stand the stares of the party in the lounge or whether she should be sheltered from the wolves by piloting her through the kitchen door to the smaller lounge on the first floor, which had more privacy.

'Good Lord,' Charles Anjorin exclaimed as he stepped back when after opening the door he was confronted by the very masculine and bespectacled face of Roy Simpson, Minister of Home Affairs, instead of the made-up face of a woman he had anticipated.

'Good Lord, what is the matter, darling?' Simpson said, still feigning the high-pitched tone of a woman. He also pretended to be genuinely surprised at the behaviour of his friend Anjorin, which sent the five politicians back to their boisterous laughing and rude remarks.

'Minister of Education, Minister of Ladies,' Badejo commented. 'Tell me one thing. Just one thing. Aren't you ever tired of them?'

They all laughed afresh, Anjorin laughing the loudest.

'Enough now,' Simpson said, putting his hat on top of the rediffusion box and proceeding to lower his bulk into one of the eight easy chairs which were delivered only the day before. Cabinet had directed in an Exco. Conclusion that the Permanent Secretary must order from the new furniture firm, that was one of the joint ventures between Government and the Jordarmenians, a set of this high-class furniture for each of the nine V.I.P. rest houses in the country. After adjusting himself in the chair Simpson proceeded to wipe the perspiration off his face. 'I'm sorry to be late, gentlemen. You cannot trust these people,' he said, looking round the room apprehensively.

'You don't need to apologize,' Kofi Kojo said, regarding the late-comer with affectionate interest. 'You were not the only one to be late. Charlie too first motored to the other side of the town looking for the Nursing Sister.'

'Minister, please!' the Minister of Education protested.

'She's out of town. She wasn't expecting him today. Or you either, Minister,' he turned round to Titus Badejo, pretending seriousness.

'Look, you chaps,' Kofi Kojo said, sipping his fifth glass of Star. 'You mustn't damage the good name of Titus. He is the only one of you rotten lot that is not fallen yet.'

'Very true, very true,' Roy Simpson commented, sipping his beer. 'Titus Badejo is the only one among us still standing. Bo, my friend, keep standing.'

'We all must encourage him. One man One wife,' Roy Simpson pronounced the much abused, much derided slogan.

'One Man One Wife be damned,' Anjorin snapped. 'All you hypocrites. I'm no hypocrite.'

'We all know. And we know your difficulties too,' Badejo commented. He lit a new cigarette.

'Thank you, my brother,' the Minister of Education said in appreciation of his colleague's understanding.

'Women Education Officers. Female students wanting Government Scholarships. Ladies wanting to supply food-stuffs to schools. What can a human male do in such circumstances?'

'My brother, you understand my problem,' Anjorin commented.

They all laughed. Roy Simpson laughed the loudest, his great expanse of belly shaking like jelly as he laughed first at Badejo's analysis and next at the admission by Charles Anjorin of his difficulties.

'How can anyone stand in such circumstances? Just tell me,' Anjorin asked of his colleagues.

'Fact is that that fellow was never once on his legs,' Roy Simpson declared. 'The fellow had been lying horizontal for years before fortune blew him to the Ministry of Education.' Again they all laughed. And again Simpson laughed the loudest.

'Gentlemen! Gentlemen please,' Kofi Kojo cried and clapped his hands in an attempt to call order of some sort amongst all the yelling going on. 'Look, we are supposed to be at the Town Hall in another half an hour. We mustn't allow people to say that we are not campaigning hard enough for Alade.'

'True, too true,' Charles Anjorin agreed. 'Gentlemen, let's be moving on to the Town Hall. And what's most important, we must arrive there sober.'

'But nearly all the people we should be addressing there are already at Dauda's rally at the Victoria Lorry Park,' Badejo observed. 'Difficult to understand these people. In spite of all the things this Party has done for them they continue to run after that rabble rouser. I cannot understand the mentality of these people,' Badejo said in an anguished voice.

At that moment they heard a distant shouting and clapping of hands over a loud-speaker system. 'That must be coming from St James' School,' Kofi Kojo observed. 'Apparently it is there that Dauda's gang are holding their own meeting and not at the Lorry Park. The Council Clerk refused to issue them a permit to use the Lorry Park, I know.'

They were all pleased about that. The Local Authority staff under the very able leadership of the £360 a year Clerk had become an arm of the Government party in their official activities. Market stalls, permits to operate taxi cabs, petty contract awards – all these essentials to keep body and soul together in the fierce struggle for existence went to men and women known to hold government party cards. The local government police and the sanitary inspectors were most ruthless in their prosecution of cases of minor offences against the public health by-laws involving members of the Opposition party while councillors and other members of the Government party were known to treat smallpox cases in their own houses without anyone thinking that anything had gone amiss.

'But how did they get into that school – St James' you say?' the Minister of Home Affairs asked seriously.

'Yes. The headmaster is a confirmed Opposition man. He will go anywhere with Dauda.'

'That's the trouble,' Education observed seriously as he recharged his glass. 'That's the trouble. All these teachers; they indoctrinate the boys they are supposed to teach. I told that Rev. Father only two days ago that unless Government is satisfied that these teachers stop their anti-Government activities, I'm going to cut the grant-in-aid to their mission schools drastically. I wish you had seen his face when he was leaving my office.' They all laughed as they imagined the confused face of the Rev. Father being told off by a Minister of State.

'Eh, you fellows – hear what that man is saying now!' Simpson alerted the others. They all listened.

'I ask you again, fellow countrymen and comrades in persecution and oppression,' the hated voice of Abdul Dauda boomed over the loudspeaker. 'Just what have they done in their twelve months in office? What have they done?'

'Nothing!' the distant shout of the crowd reached the Ministers in the lounge of the V.I.P. Rest House.

'What have they done?' again Dauda's powerful voice carried over the loudspeaker.

'Nothing!' again the crowd shouted.

'No, they *have* done something. In fact three things. And I'll tell them to you presently.'

After an interruption by a great shout of anticipation the speaker continued: 'In the first place they have increased their own salaries.'

Again there was a great shout of hate. The speaker's voice continued after the interruption: 'When they came to power each Parliamentarian earned £400 a year. Each Parliamentary Secretary, £900. And each Minister £1800 . . . What d'you think they pay themselves now? Parliamentarians, £900. Parliamentary Secretaries, £1800. And Ministers of State – listen, listen —' the speaker had to stop for the shouting of the crowd, the ventilation of their indignation and astonishment at men who paid themselves so much from public funds, to subside. 'Now the Ministers. Hear what they now pay themselves, £3000 a year! £3000, not counting mileage, gardeners' and a thousand and one other allowances . . .'

'The man is terrible,' Anjorin commented, while the distant crowd in St James' indulged in prolonged shouting. 'But how does he get these details? How does he get them?' Anjorin looked round the faces of his colleagues.

'What a question from a Minister of State!' Badejo retorted. 'From the official Estimates of course. The whole thing is published in the Estimates. You fellows will recall my proposal that the Estimates be made a secret document and that its distribution be restricted to Ministers only – wait, the wretch is at the microphone again!'

'Imagine a school teacher earning £390 before election. Now a Minister of State he earns not £780, not £1000. Not £1500. He now earns – £3000!'

'That wretch is referring to me,' Kofi Kojo said, shaking his head. 'If I get hold of his neck I'll wring it, till the life is squeezed out of his hateful body,' he threatened.

'Listen, listen —' Badejo cautioned, irritated and excited.

'You want to know what else they have done?' Dauda's voice was again on the air. 'They have increased the number of Ministers and Parliamentary Secretaries in the Cabinet. When they came to power they had eleven Ministers and seven Parliamentary Secretaries. Now there are twenty-five Ministers of State and seventeen Parliamentary Secretaries . . . (prolonged shouting) . . . Ministers of the Inner Circle. Ministers of Cabinet rank. Ministers without Portfolio. Ministers in the Ministry of this, Ministers in the Ministry of that. Do you wonder then that the budget for the Prime Minister's Office has risen from £58,000 to £195,000?' – prolonged shouting.

'You want to know the third thing they've done? Listen. They have not constructed new roads and new bridges, they have not constructed new hospitals and trained new doctors. But they have spent endless time arguing which Minister's name shall be given to which street in the new Housing Estate that was actually constructed before they came to power. Little men with little minds! Vested with power for a brief moment, they have desecrated the pages of a nation's history by giving their dishonourable names to the highways and landmarks of the nation . . .'

'Gosh, the man is a genius, damn his politics,' Simpson observed in secret admiration.

'He ought to be a professor in the University. That's where he belongs,' Kofi Kojo joined in the admiration.

'But they won't have him there,' Charles Anjorin said. 'The Universities just don't take any soap-box orator that sways the crowd this way and that.'

'Look, you fellows,' Simpson said seriously, 'I think we are underrating the power of this man Dauda. See the way he controls the crowd. I think we have to be more careful with him.'

'The man is an evil genius.'

'What I don't understand is why our boys haven't broken up that meeting,' Anjorin said. 'Why, that's what they are paid for isn't it?'

'I've told you fellows that I don't trust those boys. I think half of them are in the pay of Dauda. They get paid by both sides. I have evidence for what I'm saying.'

'Really! Then Dauda must be paying out pots and pots of money, paying his own thugs and our boys,' Anjorin observed. 'I think we shouldn't worry ourselves unduly about Dauda, while at the same time we mustn't allow ourselves to be complacent. One thing, most of the people shouting out there have no votes at all. You see they are mostly the Grammar School boys, lorry drivers, touts, and hooligans. Such of them as qualify to register failed to register. You know, the usual fear of registration having some remote connection with taxation.' Here he paused to light a cigarette. 'And Gorgeous Gregory has fixed those of them that thought that their names are on the Voters' list.'

'And one thing I say,' Simpson said, adjusting himself in the chair. 'You people, you talk too much book. Politics needs sense, not book. You see, let Dauda talk all the grammar he knows to those school boys and drivers outside. We must talk the language that our people understand.

Money. That's the language of politics. Are we spending the money in the right places? That's what I want you people to be careful about.'

'Good talk! Very good talk,' Anjorin nodded.

'I think the campaign is going on quite well in that respect – Gorgeous Gregory has fixed everything. The fellow —'

'Look,' Badejo interrupted. 'I think we must make allowance for Gorgeous Gregory's exaggerations. I myself think that we may find that some of these people take money from us and from Dauda. We must make allowance for treachery.'

'This is where the oath-taking comes in,' Anjorin said with a sparkle in his face. 'There we must give credit to Gorgeous – another genius, a perfect match for Dauda, in collaboration with Chief Odole and the Owari priest.'

'There's so much noise about the thing in the papers —' Badejo commented, sipping his current glass of stout.

'Quite! Because the thing is hurting Dauda bad – quite bad. You see Dauda had been complaining to the police that the thing was going on but the police boys pretended that there was nothing in it. The police boss himself told me the story. But when our boys began to do the thing too openly the police could no longer pretend not to know about it.'

'Just what did they do?' Simpson asked. They all wanted to know details of this thing that was hurting Dauda so badly.

'Our boys were forcing both Christians and Moslems to take the Owari oath at the shrine at Ipelo. The Vicar of St Emmanuel complained in a long report to the police. The police could no longer ignore both the church people and Dauda. So they got into their jeep on Thursday afternoon and drove to Ipelo.' Anjorin chuckled at what he was about to say next.

'Come on man, let's have it,' Simpson said, anticipating some entertainment.

'The police boys arrived at the entrance to the shrine just as three men were coming out of a taxi, carrying three white cocks. There was a queue of men carrying cocks waiting for their turn to go into the grove where the shrine was. A few of them made for the bush at the sight of the police. A few rushed into the sacred grove, somewhat out of turn. Those in the middle of their own rites became apprehensive and attempted to escape. But then the only entrance also served as exit.'

'Trapped,' Badejo said in a yawn.

'Yes, trapped completely. The Police Inspector and his men saw the fresh blood and feathers on the Owari when they went in. They looked at the men, at the priest – a toothless old man who but for this issue of the by-election had fallen into insignificance since in these days of Christianity and Islam and politics people had stopped seeking the opinion of Owari about the future. The Police Inspector asked them if they knew that they were engaged in a criminal act. He ordered the priest to describe the details of the rites. The priest first declined but then the police boys became rough with him. And the old man described the details of the oath. The words were:

'It is I, so-so-and-so, calling oh Owari. If on the day we are to elect a man to speak for our town in the big meeting at Victoria I do not cast my vote for Moses then my day will be as black as night. My way will be as bushy as the thickest forest. May my house become desolate and be overgrown with weeds. May I die a violent death with no sons and daughters to mourn my death!'

'Terrible!' Badejo shivered. They all thought it was horrible.

'Terrible. After the police boss had recorded these and a few other notes in his pocket book he ordered the old man and his converts to carry the Owari into the police jeep. The old man nearly collapsed at this suggestion which was sacrilege. He wailed a loud protest. "If anyone dares touch the Owari he will die a violent death" the old man enlightened the ignorant police chief. "Besides the Owari must never, never, never leave this grove at Ipelo." But when the Inspector gave the old man two blows of his baton on the shoulder he and the other two heaved the Owari and carried it towards the police jeep. The Police Inspector ordered them first to put it on the ground near the jeep. He then got a gallon of Gamalin-20 from a farmer in the crowd that had gathered to see what was happening. This he poured on the Owari to disinfect it from the stench of many days' accumulation of chicken blood and rotting feathers. After this the priest and the two men carried it into the jeep in which they all kept the deity company on the bumpy ride back to Newtown.' Anjorin smiled in satisfaction. He had told a good story well, he felt.

'Good Lord!' Kofi Kojo exclaimed.

'Where are they now?' Simpson wanted to know.

'Well, the old priest has been bailed. I think the men too have been bailed. The Minister of Justice has instructed the police not to proceed with the case. Unfortunately no one has been able to arrange bail for the Owari! The famous ageless deity of Ipelo is still undergoing deportation from her ancient home in Ipelo and, which is more, the outrage of forced custody on the lawn outside the office of the Superintendent at the police station in Newtown.'

Twenty-four

———————◇———————

EVEN though polling was not due to start till 8 a.m. on election day at Newtown, activities had started shortly after midnight. Indeed at the Freedom for All Party headquarters it was an all-night session for the disposition of party vans and the movement of party officials.

Rain threatened to affect the elections. Dauda's men accused Freedom for All Party supporters of being responsible for ordering the rain from the professional rain-makers. They said that the Government Party, having sunk very much in popularity, were not enthusiastic about the election and were looking for any excuse that would make voters stay away. The inconvenience of being drenched by rain and the fear of being followed by the Owari curse would together make the supporters of the Opposition Party stay away. But Gorgeous Gregory issued what he described as an official communique on behalf of the Freedom for All Party. He accused the Opposition of evil machinations and electioneering intrigues and said that in spite of the Opposition having paid fabulous sums of money to rain-makers (details of which were in possession of the Freedom for All Party) so that rain would fall in the hope that Government would be obliged to cancel the election, the election would go on. He pointed out that there was no provision in the electoral regulations for the postponement or cancellation of an election because of rain. As it happened there was much lightning, much rumbling and grumbling behind the clouds. But there was no rain.

Queues had started forming at some polling stations before 8 a.m. Moses drove from station to station where the streets were motorable, but he was obliged to trek in each case some hundred yards or so to other stations where the streets were too narrow, tortuous, or the road had become too corrugated or potholed for his car. He was dressed in a green serge 'conductor' outfit, a cross between a shirt and a jacket worn over instead of being tucked in the top of the trousers. A red 'liberty' badge was pinned to his Sekou Toure cap. He carried a walking stick which served both as a complement to his outfit as well as a third leg which he really needed on that tiring day. Gorgeous Gregory, his election agent, was truly gorgeous that day. He was dressed in a grey English suit with bowler hat, polished black shoes, and white gloves. In addition to a dud pipe which drooped at the corner of his mouth he carried an umbrella, Chamberlain fashion, with a horse tail stuck to its handle.

There was a ban on electioneering and any form of political activities within a hundred and twenty yards of any polling station on election day. In spite of this crowds of Freedom For All Party supporters cheered Moses at each station. He and Gorgeous Gregory would acknowledge the cheering of the crowd, the latter shaking his umbrella which amounted to waving the horsetail on its handle. But Moses was not happy. He knew that many people not only in Dauda's but in his own party had stayed away from the elections not so much for fear of rain or death by lightning but for fear of being rough-handled by Freedom For All Party stalwarts whom Gorgeous Gregory had organized to do just this.

They ran into Lola at one of the polling stations just before noon.

'You are looking smashing, Lola,' Moses said, truly admiring her.

'Thank you, Minister,' she said, curtsying in feigned respect.

Lola was indeed charming. To the surprise of Moses she wore a buba and iro outfit of green serge, of exactly the same material as the clothes Moses was wearing. She had on a maroon silk head tie with the folds made into an attractive design. She had a pair of maroon shoes to match.

'Do people dress so gorgeously on election day?' Moses teased her.

'Ask Mr Gregory,' she said, looking at the dandy Gorgeous Gregory. 'He should know.'

'You women. You seize every and any occasion to show off your latest fashions.'

'But sir, what I am wearing is exactly the same material as yours. Not better. And I've not yet accused you of showing off.'

'But there's a difference, my dear,' Moses said, eyeing her suspiciously.

'Yes?'

'I am the candidate. You are not.'

She laughed softly. Gorgeous Gregory too laughed. 'You are the candidate, I am not,' she repeated, looking a little serious. 'Even if I was the candidate I don't think I could have done half the things I've done today.'

'Like leaving the office to come to vote? All civil servants are to be given an hour off for voting. I know Mr McDonald would give you two.'

'But Lola has been on duty nearly all day,' Georgeous Gregory remarked. 'She is one of our key ladies. How many times have you been, Lola?'

'Five.'

'Five times to where?'

'Oh, Minister! Candidate! Chief!' she said in feigned rebuke. 'As if you don't know!'

Then he put two and two together and got it. Lola had already voted five times that day. That meant that she had visited five polling stations. At each station she had voted under a different name. And at each station she had cast not one vote but several. Moses had known of the plan to play this trick. He had opposed it and thought that it had been abandoned. And there was this pretty, respectable lady allowing herself to be used for this ingenious election fraud. Each vote was bought from the registered voter for 10/-. 5/- was paid at the conclusion of the bargain, usually a few days before election day. On election day the voter went to the polling station at which his name was on the register. After going through the processes of being checked in by the polling staff, he was given a ballot paper which he was to take inside the polling booth and drop inside one of the two boxes on which was pasted a picture of the candidate for whom he wished to vote. All voters whether or not they had been bribed went through these processes up to the stage of entering the booth. The honest voter dropped his ballot paper in the box of his choice. But the bribed voter dropped his ballot paper in his pocket. He then went out as if he had cast his vote as a good citizen. Some hundred yards away he entered a house owned by a Party supporter. There he met some half a dozen Party officials seated drinking beer. He brought out the ballot paper in his pocket and handed this over to one of these men. In return he was given the 5/- balance and thanked for a good job done. The ballot paper was added to several others recovered in a similar manner. A trusted Party supporter of status that would exempt him (or her) from being searched by the polling officials would now keep well hidden in the innermost pockets of his clothes all these ballot papers and then sally forth ostensibly to go and cast his own vote. Inside the booth he cast his vote all right. But he did more: he dumped in the box of the Party candidate all the ballot papers that had been illegally acquired.

Moses was truly amazed at the daring of the girl. 'But Lola, you did that?'

'Why not?' she laughed softly. 'And I'm going to Ward M now – let me see now, station 17. They are expecting me.'

'To repeat this thing? Tell me, where d'you keep the papers?' he asked in curiosity.

'Don't be rude, Minister,' she said coyly. Gorgeous Gregory laughed in embarrassment.

Then he understood as his eyes travelled down the contours of her breasts.

Alade Moses later heard the story of another girl who had not succeeded so well in her own mission. She was pregnant – with ballot papers, a fact that came to light when something gave way in the inner reaches of her frock and wads of ballot papers dropped from her person as she was alighting from the taxi outside the polling station. Thereupon Dauda's gang set upon her before the police came to her rescue.

After polling had closed and the polling boxes were being assembled at the Newtown Court-house preparatory to the counting of the votes, Moses heard the story of what happened to Dauda that day. Apparently Dauda had reached the polling station about an hour after polling began, amidst the cheering of his supporters. But to his dismay big political party boss Dauda was told by the polling officials that he had already voted! Yes, there it was on the register, his name, Abdul Dauda, No. 107069, ticked with a red pencil, an indication that he had voted. The names of his four wives, including one that had been bed-ridden for months, had been ticked red too. And so were the names of his sons, including the boy at that time swotting for the finals of his M.B., Ch.B. in Glasgow. Yes, according to the records they had all voted!

Moses shook his head unhappily at this story, which his friends found so interesting. He knew the foundations of another election petition had been well and truly laid.

During the counting of the votes he was hurriedly called to a conference with the Chief Electoral Officer, the Secretary of the Electoral Commission, and the Commissioner of Police in the twelve by ten room that served as the judges' chambers in the court room. Moses was told of a serious election complaint which had been addressed to the police. The police boss handed the official envelope to Moses. He slowly extracted from it the letter. He saw that it was from an expatriate official from the Ministry of Finance. No wonder the Election Commission and the police did not want to make it disappear in a hurry – he knew that a number of such complaints from Dauda's supporters had vanished without a trace:

'. . . I first drove to the polling station at the Salvation Army School in ward G at 10.45 a.m. on polling day. I was surprised when the Polling Officer told me that I was not registered to vote at that station. I went through the register with him and discovered that it was true that my name was not on his register. Yet the polling notification papers sent to me by the office of the Electoral Commission did show that this was the station where I was registered to vote.

'I checked up with the office of the Electoral Commission and discovered that someone in that office had made last minute changes in the polling arrangements and that I and my neighbours at the Government Residential Area were to vote at the St Augustine polling station. Thither I went after I had informed a few other people on the telephone about the change. I arrived there at 11.35 a.m. My name was on the register there all right. But I was told by the Polling Officer that the station had run out of ballot papers and that he was expecting another consignment from the office of the Electoral Commission before long. I called again after my dinner at 2.30 p.m. but I was told that the consignment of ballot papers had not arrived.

'When I called again at 5.30 p.m. the ballot papers still had not arrived. At this time I met a large crowd of people who, I was told, were like me wanting to cast their votes but could not do so because there were no ballot papers. This crowd appeared to me to be quite angry at the inefficient arrangements which had made it impossible for them to cast their votes.

'Someone in the crowd told me that he first came to the polling station at 9.00 a.m. and that he was told even at that time that the station had run out of ballot papers and that he and the other people waiting in the long queue should go and come back later in the day when the consignment of papers which they were expecting from the Electoral Commission would have arrived.

'I decided to make this report to the police because I feel that there are sufficient grounds to suspect that either through inefficiency or corrupt influence someone or some organization has deprived a large number of people of exercising their sacred privilege of electing through their votes the person who shall represent them in the legislature. It will be very sad indeed if in only two short years after the departure of the British who guided this model nation to true nationhood it begins to tear down the very foundations of democracy and representative government.'

He could not identify the signature of the expatriate civil servant who had stuck out his neck for a cause he believed in, the right of the individual citizen to cast his vote without let or hindrance for the candidate of his choice. No doubt a Communist or a fellow traveller, one that would not have gone though the screening of the Colonial Office in London when Britain still had responsibility for the recruitment of expatriate staff for the Colony.

'What are we going to do about this, Minister?' the Police Commissioner asked, his face creased with anxiety.

'What you are to do about it? Don't ask me. I'm a candidate, not a member of the Electoral Commission,' Moses said, tired and annoyed. He left the two men and walked out of the room, his unhappiness shown clearly on his face.

'Ah, Minister,' someone whispered to him as he re-entered the hall where the counting was still going on. 'Congratulations. We have won with a comfortable majority.'

'Thank you,' Moses muttered, with little interest.

'You're well sir?'

'Very well, thank you,' he said without conviction. 'But I'm tired. I think I want to go home now.'

'But sir, you must wait for the official announcement of the results. It shouldn't be long now.'

'No, I'd rather not. Please get the driver to bring my car round to the side entrance.'

On his way home the ghost of the expatriate voter done out of his vote haunted his thoughts. The way his supporters had cheated Dauda and his family of their votes worried him. Again he convinced himself that the foundation of another election petition against him was truly laid. Back home he drugged himself and deep sleep mercifully, if only temporarily, relieved him of his unhappiness.

One of the six cases of election irregularities highlighted under the big headline of 'Government Party Rigged Election' on the front page of the Opposition paper filled his cup of unhappiness to overflowing the following morning. 'They say that he scored 13,684 and that our own candidate scored 8,912. This makes a total of 22,596. But there are only 16,451 names on the Voters List. So more people have voted in Newtown than were registered to vote. In their hurry to rig the election the Government Party and their stooges the electoral officers had not taken even the most elementary precaution to cover their dirty, hideous trail. This time they will not get away with this daylight robbery.'

Twenty-five

—————————◇—————————

FIVE days after the by-election Alade Moses lay sleepless and restless in bed in the Moyamba Rest House. It was mid-morning but he stayed in bed in the hope that the sleep that had eluded him after the long night motoring from Newtown would come in the morning.

Then the telephone rang. He fumbled for the receiver on the cabinet near the bed. It was Gloria. 'Listen,' she said, her voice quavering with anxiety. 'You must leave at once. They are coming.'

'Why, who, Glor?' he asked, frightened.

'Don't go back to Newtown. Don't go by the main road. You must —'

'Glor, Glor, Glor,' Alade Moses cried as he fiddled frantically with the instrument after Gloria's voice had faded into inaudibility in the middle of a sentence. He dialled her number frantically. It was engaged. He sought the assistance of the telephone operator. She was sorry, the line was out of order. He pronounced a terrible curse on the P. & T. as he banged the telephone in fury.

He had come to this relatively quiet rest house that he might truly have a rest from the strain of the electioneering and from the anxiety that the post election situation was fast creating. He remembered the words of the doctor who the day before had advised the trip. 'You will just drop dead if you don't go away for a week's rest – today. It is my duty to warn you in my dual capacity as your friend and your doctor.' In spite of drugs smuggled out to him by Gloria from the hospital he had not been sleeping at all even after the election. Apart from his roaming mind the activities of his ministerial colleagues and political associates had not helped matters. These had made the occasion of the by-election an opportunity for turning his new and modern house at Newtown into a sort of hide-out for themselves and their current girl friends. Here they drowned themselves in crates of beer and stout, gin and whisky. Only Gloria and Chief Odole and his faithful steward Patrick were privy to the plan for the retreat in Moyamba. He had to leave Newtown late at night – a journey like this was best undertaken at night. He had slept a little during the uneventful ride in the Mercedes 300S. But that was all the rest he was destined to get. For sleep simply eluded him for the remaining four hours of night on arrival at Moyamba Rest House.

And now he must leave. Why, he did not know. Where for he did not know immediately. But not Newtown; and not Victoria – intuition told him that.

The trouble against which Gloria warned him started in Newtown just before noon that day. An ancient Hillman Minx, driven by Geo Abyssinia, who had since defected to the Opposition party, allegedly after he had been bribed by Dauda, refused to give way to a Land Rover coming from the right at the roundabout near the entrance to the town. The Land Rover 65W17 belonged to the Government Party, one of the fourteen that had recently come back victorious from the by-election campaign. Its driver was thus armed with the power of both the law, which stipulated that motorists must stop for vehicles on the right at roundabouts, and of working for the Government Party. He pressed hard on the throttle in hot pursuit of the offending vehicle. He overtook it most dangerously and then stopped his own vehicle in the middle of the road, thereby forcing the Hillman to stop. To the surprise of the driver and the six stalwarts that jumped out of 65W17 Abyssinia peeped out of the Hillman and shouted insults at them and at Alade Moses whom they served. This was clearly too much. They dragged him out of his car and beat him up, his exalted position as Principal of the Grammar School notwithstanding. They then forced him into their Land Rover and drove away, amidst the yelling of the crowd that had formed at the scene.

The route of 65W17 passed in front of the head-quarters of the Opposition Party, a thing which the kid-nappers of Geo Abyssinia had overlooked in their retreat from the traffic confusion which they had created where they had taken the law into their own hands. The van was only some thirty yards from this headquarters building before the driver noticed that 'Trust in God' had been parked right in the middle of the road. Now 'Trust in God', a Bedford truck that had known many owners, was known to have been acquired by Dauda's party just before the by-election. The police were known to have withdrawn its road-worthiness certificate a few days before the by-election and by all reasonable calculation it ought not to be on the road, certainly not in the middle of the road that day. But there it was, there, indicating to 65W17 that was now being forced into a screeching stop that trouble was imminent, very imminent.

It started with empty beer bottles being hurled at 65W17 from all directions even before it had come to a full stop. The driver staggered out of the vehicle and at once became the meeting point of several bottles, one of which landed on his head and knocked him down, senseless. Two of the thugs who jumped out of the van suffered the same fate. At a whistle signal from Dauda's first floor office in the party building, the throwing of bottles stopped. Some ten or so men came out and invaded 65W17 and proceeded to teach the four men of the enemy still remaining inside the same lesson that they had taught Abyssinia. Two of the boys carried away Abyssinia's senseless form for treatment in the party building.

Flushed with victory, Dauda's men packed themselves into 'Trust in God' and drove towards the headquarters of Freedom For All Party. The boys at that headquarters had not yet recovered from the surprise of the way in which Dauda's men had reacted to the incident at the roundabout and had declared what looked like total war. They were worried about the fate of their comrades in the kidnapping team now themselves kidnapped and most likely under torture at the enemy's headquarters building. They had tried to contact Chief Alade Moses. They were disappointed he was not in. No one appeared to know where he was. The Minister of Local Government told the spokesman from the party headquarters that he would contact the Police Superintendent and get Dauda and his gang arrested. They were therefore very surprised indeed when Dauda's men who they thought had been arrested and locked up by the police now arrived in 'Trust in God' to invade them in their own headquarters.

The battle of the thugs raged at the Freedom For All Party headquarters with fury. Weapons of a wide range were used. The defenders started with empty bottles. The invaders answered back bottle for bottle. Then the attackers got bolder. They jumped out of 'Trust in God' and in spite of the rain of bottles, advanced holding matchets which they wielded most frighteningly. A number of the defenders ran into the inner security of the building while a few others stood still flinging the blood-letting bottles. After some time those that had retreated came back with their own matchets. Then the real battle started. And it went on for over an hour, with casualties on both sides, with confusion in the immediate vicinity of the battleground, and with a general sense of trouble and fear pervading the general atmosphere in Newtown.

By the time the police came, the invading thugs had left in their truck, leaving behind three of their number captives of the defending army. The police ransacked the party headquarters building and arrested five of the eleven party men they found there who, along with the injured captives of the invading army, they bundled into their jeep and drove to the police station.

Back at their own headquarters Dauda's men were shocked to discover that the police had paid them a visit in their absence, ransacked the building, removed a number of documents and arrested a number of men who had come in since they left for the Freedom For All party headquarters operation. This unfriendly act on the part of the police infuriated Dauda's men. They made for the police station without much ado. At the sight of 'Trust in God' and of the stalwarts jumping down from it, the police sergeant behind the desk at the duty office thought of personal safety before duty. He fled. Two other police constables at the station and three men who were at that time being interrogated by the sergeant also fled in panic. The panic spread to the office of the police superintendent. He escaped through the rear exit. It spread to the nearby market where men and women ran helter-skelter. Dauda's men ransacked the police station, freed their own men and some other people who were in custody for offences that the police were still investigating. They then drove back in their faithful 'Trust in God.'

After a couple of hours rest and regrouping of their forces, Dauda's men struck again that night, and once more their target was the building of the Freedom For All Party headquarters.

Again they were not expected. Both the party boys in the building and the bosses who exercised remote control from the security of the new house built for Alade Moses had hoped that the earlier effort would have exhausted them and that the police reinforcement expected from Victoria would have arrived. Unfortunately it had not.

It was difficult to tell the identity of the leader of the invading team in the dark but it appeared that there had been a change in command. The defenders in any case did not wait to establish who was who in the attacking force. They fled. The attackers, finding little resistance, proceeded to smash up doors and windows, chair, tables and desks. They finally set the building on fire.

The new building of Alade Moses in Newtown was attacked in the early hours of the following morning. In spite of its being only a few weeks old, the house was quite used to vehicles of all sorts arriving at awkward hours of the night. The noise of the three trucks drawing up on the spacious drive was in no way different from the noise of party trucks arriving from some overnight assignment or bringing some important constituency member to see the Minister. But moments later, a short piercing blast from the whistle of the police constable on guard duty warned of trouble. The entrance porch light and two other lights that were still on in some of the rooms went out. This was followed immediately by shrieks and shouts of fright from various parts of the building. More people were awakened by the noise of those running here and there in panic along the corridors without any definite idea of which way led to safety. In the confusion, Ministers of State and their body-guards collided with each other and with women in scanty bedclothes, all seeking safety from the enemy of uncertain identity and strength. The one man in the building who remembered that in case of emergency one should ring the police did manage to get to the telephone. But it was dead. Apparently the attackers had disconnected the telephone immediately before disconnecting the electricity.

In the light of lanterns and torches the attackers went to work. They assaulted the building with axes, matchets, and sticks. They smashed doors and windows, forcing some of these off their hinges. They went from room to room, destroying furniture and pictures hanging on the wall. They wrought complete destruction on a building which was till then the show piece of Newtown. The inmates had all succeeded in escaping into the bush out on to the road to Victoria.

Three more houses of Freedom For All Party supporters including Chief Odole's, were attacked that night. In each of them the attackers had given sufficient warning for the inmates to flee. Two of them were mud buildings of little strength and value. These did not take long to demolish. But both Chief Odole and his house offered some resistance. In spite of the tearful entreaties of his household, the old man refused to leave. He was badly beaten up by the attackers, and the house partly destroyed.

The following morning the papers carried reports of widespread acts of lawlessness and arson in the main towns of Afromacoland. Houses and cars of known supporters of the government party were reported attacked and set on fire. Many people were reported beaten up, a good number injured and admitted to hospital. The opposition paper claimed that seven men had been killed, including Chief the Honourable Franco-John, Minister of Agriculture.

'But what's Government doing about all this?' Norman Bruce asked, stroking his whiskers. 'If someone doesn't arrest the situation at once, the country is finished. Why, no investors will look at the country again.' He took a long pull at his beer. He then looked through the window. 'Just look at that,' he said, excited. 'Another one on fire. My God.'

'That looks like the house of the Minister of Information, at least it is in that direction,' Theo George said. 'Looks as if more people are behind this than the men of Dauda's gang.'

'Without doubt, man,' Norman Bruce agreed.

'I hear Dauda has been arrested,' Geoff Shepherd observed. 'But as you say the whole thing looks more than the handwork of his boys.'

'You blokes don't know these boys,' Bruce said sadly. 'One would have expected the secret intelligence of your friends in the Government to have discovered the activities of the China-trained revolutionaries. Of course they are behind the whole thing. Trained to subvert properly elected governments. On the payroll of Communist countries through their embassies. My God!'

Theo George looked through the window of the sitting room of Geoff Shepherd's A3 bungalow where the three of them had been drinking, following the hour to hour development in the situation. 'I hear that rogue is dead – that one that goes by the name of one of the sixteenth century popes,' Bruce observed, still looking through the window.

'Gorgeous Gregory. No one will mourn him,' Geoff Shepherd observed.

'Roasted alive, I hear,' Norman Bruce continued. 'First sprayed with petrol. Then set ablaze. My God! I'm sick inside.'

'Terrible thing, you know,' George said, refilling his glass. 'You know the equipment for spraying cocoa trees against the black pod disease? They fill the wretched thing with petrol instead of the specification Gamalin 20. Then they direct the jet not on cocoa trees but on human beings and houses and vehicles. Then they set their victims ablaze. Good God!'

After some moments silence Norman Bruce asked: 'What about your friend, Geoff?'

'Alade Moses? I imagine he's fled. The obvious thing to do in the circumstances,' Geoff said, somewhat indifferently.

'Most gallant of him eh. That wretched by-election in his constituency sparked off the whole thing. One would have expected a man of honour to face the consequences of his political dishonesty. Never pays anywhere. Once you begin to fiddle with the ballot box —'

'Actually the rigging of the by-election was just the immediate cause of the trouble,' Theo George cut in. 'The people were fed up with the corruption and deceit of the Government. They were merely waiting for an opportunity to kick them out. And the rigging of the by-election in Newtown just happened to be the last straw.'

At that point they all saw the newspaper boy labouring up the drive on his ancient bicycle. *Sentinel:* special afternoon edition. Latest Revolution News,' the boy cried in between breaths.

Shepherd snatched the copy the boy held out to him and all three of them scanned through the first page.

'Ministers on the Run,' the first headline screamed.

'Gorgeous Gregory Roasted by Angry Villagers,' another announced.

'Arrest of Opposition Leader declared Contravention of Human Rights,' a third declared.

All three of them read the news eagerly:

'Nemesis has caught up with them, these plunderers of the wealth of the nation. They are now on the run, fleeing from the just anger of the electorate whose sacred trust they have betrayed. They are now scurrying like rats, Ministers of State who used their positions of trust to build mansions for themselves and for their girl friends . . .

'Reported Dead: Chief the Honourable Franco-John, Minister of Agriculture, and Deputy Leader of the Government Party.

'Reported missing, believed hiding in some village in the Moyamba District, Chief the Honourable Titus Badejo, Minister of Local Government. Chief the Honourable Alade Moses, former Minister of Works, and Government Party candidate in the recent by-election in the Newtown North Constituency, the result of which sparked off the disturbances . . .

'Arrested at the Sogo-Afromaco border for attempting to enter Sogoland without proper travel documents: Mr Rowland Anjorin, Minister of Education . . .'

'B.B.C. news, you chaps,' Shepherd announced as he dived for his three wave transistor radio on the sideboard in the dining room. He brought it back to the sitting room, fumbling with the controls. The voice came on in the middle of a news item about Vietnam. Then there was something about the barking of the Security Council at the goings on in South Africa. Finally came the news they all were anxious to hear: 'Reports from Afromacoland confirm that the riots which started yesterday in the provincial city of Newtown have spread into Victoria the capital and other cities. Government and private properties have been destroyed and many lives lost. Brazzaville Radio monitored through Paris has confirmed an earlier French News Agency report that the Minister killed this morning by villagers in the Moyamba District has been identified as Allah-Day Moses, who was Minister of Works in the government of Christopher Bandelay O'Gunn. The whereabouts of Mr O'Gunn himself are still unknown. Meanwhile the Voice of Afromacoland, which has been off the air since nineteen hours G.M.T. yesterday, came on the air shortly before the beginning of this bulletin with music. This news comes to you from the B.B.C. in London —'

Theo George noticed that Geoff Shepherd had walked away from the radio at the announcement of the death of Alade. Norman Bruce had poured himself another glass of stout. George turned the set to the 'Voice of Afromacoland' wavelength. It was playing music. He left it there and went back to fix himself a drink too. All three of them thought the same thing – Alade Moses. But they did not speak to each other. Presently the music stopped. Then silence. Then the radio played the National Anthem. After a few moments a strange, husky voice said: 'My fellow countrymen and women, this is Lieut.-Col. Abel Jonas, Commander of the Second Battalion of the Afromacoland Army. I speak to you tonight at a very sad moment in the history of our nation. You have all been witness to the tragic events of the last twenty-four hours in which many properties have been destroyed, many people injured, and a number of lives lost. You all have watched the inability of the civilian government, charged with responsibility for the maintenance of law and order, to arrest the situation which is growing worse from hour to hour. It is now obvious that law and order has broken down. To prevent a further deterioration in this very bad situation the National Army has decided to take over the administration of the country till such time as it considers the situation justifies a return to civilian government. When that time comes such a government will be elected by the people freely exercising their vote without the gross abuse to which elections have been subjected within the short space of time since we started our existence as an independent nation. I have been chosen by my colleagues in the three armed forces to lead this military government. I have accepted to serve in this very high office deeply conscious of the very heavy responsibility it entails. I solemnly pledge to you my countrymen and women my determination to discharge this responsibility honestly and diligently, with the interest of the nation first and foremost in my mind. We should together ask for divine guidance in the common task of retrieving our fatherland from the depth of degradation to which it had been plunged by self-seeking politicians to the height of prosperity, happiness for all our peoples, and dignity in the world community of nations. The Military Government of Afromacoland will honour existing treaties and will pursue a policy of non-alignment in the issues that divide the world. It in turn hopes that other nations will observe its national integrity and co-operate with it in its effort to bring the nation back on its feet. Long live Afromacoland.'

262   6   1927